SNOW GLOBE

SYREN NIGHTSHADE

Disclaimers

This story is a work of fiction. Names, characters, places, and incidents are the product of the author's imagination and/or are used fictitiously. Any resemblance to actual events, locales, or persons, living or dead, is completely coincidental.

Copyright © 2024 by Syren Nightshade

The reproduction, scanning, uploading, printing, or distribution of this story without the author's permission is a theft of the author's intellectual property.

Trigger/Content Warnings

- Familial Illness & Death
- Familial Disappearance
- Child Abandonment
- Medical Trauma
- Violence & Gore

1

The tips of Claire's fingers were going numb, but it had nothing to do with the cold.

It was very warm in Ash's car- he had started running the heat for her before he even arrived at her apartment building. And she was still wearing her gloves, even after almost forty-five-minutes of him driving them down dark, tree-lined backroads. Her coat was buttoned all the way up. She could feel the heated seat through the thick fabric of her coat. Ash had asked her four times on their way to the market if she was warm enough. She had started to sweat... but she suspected the temperature in the car wasn't entirely to blame.

His concern didn't annoy her- She found it endearing. She had mentioned how easily she got cold in Winter several times since they had met. Technically, it was true. She *did* get cold easily. More accurately, though, she just hated Winter. She tried to leave her home as little as possible when the snow began to fall. She kept her apartment in a constant golden hour, with candles lit day & night and blankets thrown over every piece of furniture with a seat or a ledge. *Warm* meant *safe*. And Ash may as well have appointed himself her personal protector for the evening.

She watched him pass by another empty parking spot near the end of the gravel lot. "You could have pulled into that one," she said.

"It's okay," he replied. "I'll find us a closer one."

She swallowed and adjusted her gloves. He didn't need to put this much effort into finding them a spot closer to the market building. The fact that he was trying so hard left a curious taste in her mouth, straddling the line between sweet and saccharine. But less than a minute later, they found a navy SUV with a pair of seven-foot pine trees strapped to the roof vacating a spot near the building. Ash pulled in as the SUV drove away, trees jiggling merrily as the vehicle made its way out of the lot.

He turned to her as he put the car in park and turned off the engine. "See? I told you." He gave her another one of his lopsided smiles.

Claire directed her smile into her lap as she reached for her seatbelt, trying to hide the blush she knew was coming to her cheeks. He was charming, in a very optimistic, carefree way. Luck just seemed to follow him around.

Forty-five minutes was a long drive for a first date. But you couldn't say no to Ash- not when he flashed that smile at you. When he was swept up in an idea, he had a way of getting anyone he spoke to swept up in it, too. Even if that idea involved a long drive and time spent outside in the frigid December dark.

He got out of the driver's seat and stepped outside, snow-dampened gravel whispering under his boots. He came around and opened Claire's door for her. He extended his hand- "You ready?"

"Yep." She placed her hand in his and hopped out of the car. She could already hear the endless chatter coming from inside the Christmas Market building. The big, barn-like structure was adorned with festive signposts and draped with oversized cedar garland. String lights were hung everywhere, countless tiny bulbs bursting against the blue-black sky like kitschy stars. Freshly-cut trees spilled from around the far corner of the building, leaning against the weathered wood and waiting to be picked up and taken home. A handful of people, broken off into pairs or small families, milled around the parking lot and outside the building. They all smiled- into their brown paper shopping bags, into their steaming cups, into each other's faces.

"I told you," Ash teased, inching closer to her, "I'm going to make you enjoy Winter, whether you like it or not."

She did her best to suppress another grin as she felt him playfully poke her arm. Somewhere in the back of her mind, she already knew she wasn't going to win this battle. But she refused to give him the satisfaction.

2

"So which one do you want?"

Claire giggled again. *"Stooop."*

Ash would do no such thing. She was too cute when she giggled like that. "No way. Any one you want," he repeated. "Flowers are basic. Real gentlemen buy their dates trees."

"Oh, do you know any, then?" she asked over her shoulder. Ash raised a quizzical eyebrow. "Real gentlemen, I mean."

He slammed a fist to his heart and staggered backwards in a show of melodrama. She giggled again. He feigned a dying gasp. "Don't test me," he said lightly. "I'll do it. I'll buy you the biggest tree they have. See if I don't."

"It wouldn't fit in my apartment, Casanova."

"That's okay, you could keep it at my place."

She half-scoffed. "So you're buying *yourself* a tree, then."

"Not at all. I'm giving you a place to keep *your* tree. You can even decorate it however you want."

"You wouldn't want that- I like the cute ornaments. Lots of pink. Things that look like tiny desserts. Really girly stuff."

"That's okay. I don't mind having a girly tree in my living room."

"Not as long as I come over to enjoy it, is that it?"

He let a small laugh escape him. He shrugged. "I mean..."

She hummed in a way that was probably meant to sound skeptical.

Their breath left their lips in faint puffs of mist. The cold put a rosiness into Claire's freckled cheeks. He liked her freckles. And he liked the way her eyes crinkled when he made her laugh... Which he tried to do constantly.

"Just let me know if you get too cold," he said again as they strolled through another line of trees. "We can go inside whenever you're ready."

Part of him knew that he was being overbearing. But it was hard not to keep checking in when it earned him a smile- the kind of smile that started with her pursing her lips for a split-second, begrudging- every time he did. "I'm okay," she said, eyes on the ground.

It made him feel better, focusing all of his energy on her. Trying to anticipate what she needed. Keeping an eye on what drew *her* eye.

He backtracked a couple steps as he noticed Claire shaking her foot.

"Everything okay?"

"Yeah, just a flyer or something stuck to my shoe."

He dropped to one knee. "Allow me." He pretended not to notice her smirking and rolling her eyes as he peeled the damp, ragged-edged paper from her boot. An indeterminable number of grimy boot prints marred the black and white face looking back at him beyond recognition. Snippets of a description were vaguely legible under the muck- "6'2"," "-ght brown hair," "last seen," "-black jacket and striped scarf-"

"Everything okay?"

Ash looked up at the sound of Claire's voice. "Yeah," he replied. "All good." He rose to his feet, crumpling the *Missing Person* poster in his hand and dropped it back on the ground. It was from four years ago and past the point of legibility. It couldn't be of any use to anyone, now.

3

Christmas market. Meat market.
The humans wander the Market like ants.
Many humans.
Many fears. Far away fears.
Warmth. Light. Pack. The fear is doused. The noises make the fear quiet. Far away. Far away fear has far away scent. Too far away to hunt.
The scent of fear is the scent of a wound.
I smelled them the instant they came.
His fear pulses. Steady. It thins when he nears her. He breathes on purpose. He thinks about breathing on purpose. The high-pitched taste of his fear is stuck like forever mist at the back of his mind. It teases the edge of my tongue. He *must* breathe. Memory has its hand around his throat. He remembers the sound of lungs struggling to fill. He remembers tubes curving. Choking like roots. He fears suffocation because he has seen it. He runs from it. Even now.
Her fear is sickly rich. She tries to melt herself. From the outside. From the inside. From his side. She never succeeds. She cannot push the cold from her bones. It was planted there too young. Seeded too deep. It will never leave her. And yet she tries. I can smell it. The *don't leave me* wrapped in her flesh. Marinating her muscles. Staining her marrow. Sitting like meat in a cellar. She cannot flee the dark any more than she can flee the cold.

I watch them walk through the trees. Stalk them. Watch them look to each other. Look away. Watch them walk inside.

The hunger drips from between my teeth.

Both would be delicious alone. But they did not come alone.

I am hungry. It is cold.

I do not feel the cold.

But they will.

4

The interior of the market was bright in every sense of the word.

Claire held an ornament delicately between the pads of her fingers. She could feel how thin it was through her gloves. She worried she might break it if she wasn't careful. The red ball had a metallic sheen under the slanted streaks of silver glitter. Ash chattered obliviously beside her, debating with himself on the merits of the gifts he had already purchased. As Claire had learned, he had made a very conscious, very adamant decision to gift his friends and family with *experiences* this year, rather than items. He had promptly failed at every turn.

She didn't mind his rambling. She liked listening to him chatter. She liked hearing his voice next to her.

"What *do* your Christmases usually look like?" he asked, interrupting himself. "If you celebrate, I mean."

She gingerly replaced the ornament on the hook. "Um... I do, I guess," she replied. "My family usually does something."

"'Something'?"

"Yeah- like, we'll do a whole Christmas dinner and a little gift exchange after. But that's about it. We don't go overboard or anything." Christmas was small for her family. *Subdued*. It had been since she was small. It felt wrong to be too cheerful during the holidays. It felt inappropriate to smile too much.

"Going overboard is half the fun," Ash protested. He hovered closer to her. She let him.

"For some people, I guess." She swallowed and pulled at the tips of her glove. "Is that what your family does? Goes overboard?"

He blew through pursed lips. "I mean, I wouldn't say that. We make a thing of it, sure- we do some baking together, we put a bunch of decorations up inside... outside, too. Sometimes we'll ship cookies out to each other- the ones we make, I mean. And we have this thing we do on Christmas Eve where we'll order takeout and watch a Christmas movie, and all of us just eat dinner around the couch. Then on Christmas morning, we'll make this big breakfast for everyone- we'll host each other most of the time, so it ends up being a pretty full house-"

"So you go overboard."

The corners of his mouth quirked up, but he kept talking. "*Aaand* we'll do the whole present-opening thing right before that... There are usually a few kids in the house, so we *have* to do it first thing in the morning. Naturally."

"Naturally."

"And we have a big turkey dinner, too. Very standard stuff."

"I see." Something bubbly and warm made its way from her stomach to her head. Traditions on top of traditions... It sounded whimsical and foreign.

"Oh-" he added, "And I guess it's not really *on* Christmas, but we do this thing where we make gingerbread houses. It's not like... a *contest*, exactly. But it gets pretty competitive."

She giggled. "So you're like, sabotaging each other's cookies?"

"Oh, definitely. Stealing each other's decorations. Messing with building materials. Sending gingerbread assassins. One hundred percent."

"That's very *Holiday Spirit* of you," she laughed. Imagining Ash going full-throttle on a gingerbread house, bickering with a kitchen full of family delighted her. "That sounds fun. I've never made a gingerbread house."

She suddenly felt his hand on her arm. She turned to find him frozen to the spot, bewildered. "*No*," he said. "You did *not* just say that."

"I've never made one," she repeated with a shrug.

"Oh, no," he said slowly. "Oh, that won't do. That won't do *at all*."

"I don't-"

"You're making a gingerbread house this year," he told her. "You're coming over next week- or I'll come to you, that's fine, too- or we'll rent a kitchen-"

"How do you *rent a kitchen-*?"

"-and you're making a gingerbread house. I don't care," he added when she started to protest, "we're doing this for you. It's done. It's a done deal."

She blinked. He was doing it again- that damn smile of his. "I mean, I can pick up a kit-"

"No. No, absolutely not. We're doing the entire thing from scratch. We're drafting the design-"

"'Drafting the design'."

"-Making the cookies, putting it together, decorating it... We're doing it. You *need* to do it at least once." He hesitated as they reached the end of the line of stalls. "...If you want to, I mean."

She pressed her lips together to keep herself from grinning like a fool. "Okay."

She could feel him beaming at her. He glanced behind them, back at the hot chocolate stall they had passed earlier. "It looks like the line is shorter, now," he said, nodding at the stall. "I'll go get you one. You keep looking, I'll catch up-"

Her heart jumped into her throat. "No-" her hand reflexively shot out and grabbed his arm. She immediately dropped it, embarrassed. After a few uncomfortable seconds, she smothered the panic and recovered her composure. "...I'll go with you." She tried to sound as nonchalant as she could.

Ash flashed a quick look at her hand, stuck awkwardly at her side. He smiled at her, slipped his bare hand into her gloved one, and guided her back the way they came.

Claire's stomach fluttered.

That damn smile of his.

5

Claire held the disposable cup with both hands wrapped around it so tightly that her fingers were interlaced at the tips. Ash doubted that she could feel anything through the paper and the padding of her gloves. But she still held the hot chocolate as if it was warming her palms. It was cute.

They had taken their drinks outside. There were too many people inside; Claire had made an offhanded comment about it being overwhelming. He watched the tip of her nose grow rosier the longer they strolled. He hoped the heavy chill in the air wasn't uncomfortable for her.

"Are you sure you don't want to sit in the car?" He could at least turn the heat on for her there.

"No, I'm okay."

There were no benches in sight, so they wandered aimlessly through the string-lit parking lot and the outskirts of the market building. He was still trying to hang on to the glow of Claire agreeing to see him again. He was finding it difficult- the feeling kept slipping away from him, getting lost in the thoughts that crept into the lulls in their conversation. It frustrated him. He didn't *want* to be distracted.

They had all brought gingerbread houses to the ICU this week. His paternal Aunt, her kids, his mom, his brother and sister... all of them crowded into a clinically lit hospital room, talking over each other and making too much noise around a single bed.

It should have been a sweet gesture. It should have felt good, bringing a part of Christmas to his Grandmother. Just because she couldn't be with the rest of the family didn't mean she should be alone. But it didn't feel good. It felt *wrong*. The tubes coming out of her veins like bulky marionette strings were wrong. The tubes sprouting from her throat were wrong.

Ash should have been smiling and joking with everyone else at her bedside. He tried to. He did his best to pretend. But she wasn't supposed to look like that.

He had had a nightmare about those plastic tubes again last night. They twisted themselves around his wrists and forcibly wriggled into his veins, crawling up his arms under his flesh. One slipped down his throat like a hollowed out snake; it kept plunging deeper and deeper into his body, until it started to feel like a second spine. He woke up gasping, with tears on his face.

His fears made him feel selfish. Not his fear of losing his grandmother, or seeing her in pain- that fear was normal. It was a fear on someone else's behalf. It couldn't be selfish. What felt selfish was sitting across from the foot of her bed, watching one of the people he loved most in the world struggle to breathe, and fearing for himself. Fearing that the same disease that had waited in his grandmother's body for decades, baked in from conception, was lying in wait in his own body, too.

No. Stop thinking about it.

He couldn't bear to think about it. It was too close to the edge of the dark.

"I saw a stall with a kind of *build-your-own-wreath* menu inside." He tapped his own empty cup against his thigh. "We can take a look when you're ready to go back in, if you want."

Claire smiled. "That sounds fun."

He had bought her the most excessive, overindulgent hot chocolate that money could buy. A pair of large, cube-shaped marshmallows still floated in chocolate and half-melted whipped cream. Sprinkles clung to the sides of the cup, scattered all the way up to the rim. She wasn't done with it yet, and wouldn't be for a while longer.

He watched her take another slow sip. He saw her shoulders sink as she let the warmth settle into them. He started glancing around for another distraction- something to comment on- and felt a twinge of guilt at his own desperation. This quiet moment with her *should* feel comfortable. But the quiet was giving his mind an opportunity to return to the hospital room.

Anything but that.

He wracked his brain, latching onto the first tactless thing he could find. "So... at the party. What made you say yes to giving me your number?" he asked. "What made you say yes to going on a date with me?"

She didn't answer right away. He tried not to cringe as he watched her think it over. It was true that he wanted to know the answer. *Of course he did.* But he knew better than to be so direct.

"...You sparkle."

He stopped in his tracks. He tried and failed to swallow an incredulous guffaw. "...Did you *actually* just say-?"

She stuttered. "I was going to explain-"

"*No, please,* go ahead-"

She pressed her lips together. "You're at home in any room," she answered after another pause. "We have a lot of mutual friends and acquaintances, but I don't think I've ever heard anyone say anything even *slightly* bad about you. I don't think I've heard of a single person who doesn't like you. You seem like you could be friends with anyone."

"Here I was, thinking you were just *hardcore* Team Edward."

She smirked into her cup. "...My friend told me I'd like you."

He didn't have to ask which she was talking about. "And was she right?"

She hid behind the cup, downing the last of her drink and eating the marshmallows as neatly as she could, given their size. "...Obviously," she murmured.

It was Ash's turn to smile. He had an overwhelming urge to kiss her. *God, she's cute.* He extended his hand towards her. "Here, I'll take that." She instinctively handed him the cup. He hadn't thought to look for a garbage can before he made the offer- there were none around that he could see. He stacked her cup in his and resigned himself to carrying them around for the foreseeable future. "I'll have to thank Amanda next time I see her."

Her smile, suppressed as it was, was infectious.

Neither of them spoke. It was quiet again. His mind itched looking for something to say. His eyes darted from one thing to another, searching for something to comment on... anything to keep the thoughts of his grandmother and her plastic tubes in the dark corners of his mind, where they belonged.

They rounded the corner of the building and he saw it.

A huge grin started to spread across his face. "No..."

It was too perfect.

In a small clearing ahead of the trees, a carriage stood primly in the snow. A coach sat at the front of the vehicle, leaning over to pat the rumps of the two sleek, chestnut-brown horses in front of him. One of them whinnied and kicked a hoof through the snow, shaking a confetti of snowflakes from their mane. Benches upholstered in snow-dusted red velvet sat inside the carriage, their emptiness a picturesque invitation. A small lantern was affixed to either end of the rearmost bench, giving off a warm, romantic glow.

Ash turned and beamed at Claire.

6

She thinks about petting the horses. She almost does. He watches her almost touch them. He marks it. Remembers. He keeps his eyes sharp. Like a hunter. But he is not hunting her.

I can taste the *protect* dripping through his chest. He wants a distraction. To make memories flee. He wants her. She wants him. They stay close to each other. He gives money to the driver. They do not stray from each other. The fear dampens as the space between them shrinks. I still find the fatty sweet and salt-bitter scents on the wind.

Why do humans fear being alone?

Alone is quiet. Alone is peace. Alone is a belly full of blood and meat still stuck between your teeth. Alone is not needing to share your territory. Alone is not needing to fight for prey. Alone is pleasure.

I smell the chocolate in them. It muffles the juniper berry tang of nerves. Their voices are distant. The hiss of ice-coated branches is louder. He puts his hand on her back. He helps her into the carriage. Thick water drips from my maw. Makes tiny puddles in the snow.

There are no horses. There is no carriage.
They will not remember the face of the driver.
There is no driver.
They will not see me stalking.

7

The carriage wheels rolled new grooves into the old ones, re-impressing the tracks that had started to fill with snow. The path was smooth. The trot of the horses created a pleasant jostle as they pulled deeper into the forest, pretty snow-brushed trees embracing them from either side. Ash found himself impressed with just how well the driver maneuvered the animals; every time Ash had convinced himself that the trees were too dense and that there was no possible way forward, they took a gentle, hidden curve or managed to slip between two trees with mere inches to spare.

Claire looked happy. He caught himself stealing glances at her as often as he could. She seemed perfectly content to ride in companionable silence.

He wished he could be, too.

He caught his hand tapping the edge of the carriage again. He clenched his fist in another effort to stop it. "If you could choose any name for yourself," he ventured, "what would it be?"

"Oh..." She furrowed her brow. "I never really thought about it..." Most people hadn't, in Ash's experience. Most people never had a reason to. But he was always surprised to hear the answers that people gave him. "Claire feels good. But if I *had* to change it..."

"You don't have to. That's a fair answer."

She paused. "Clara?" she suggested. "It sounds a little more elegant than Claire."

"You think so?"

"I've always really liked the name Kayleigh. Not as a name for me, though. It doesn't feel like me. I think maybe if I have a daughter one day, I'd like to name her Kayleigh."

Ash's lips curved. He liked the sound of Kayleigh.

"*Oh-*" she gasped, turning towards him. "*Trixie*. I *love* that nickname. I always have. Short for Beatrice."

"Not 'Bea*trix*'?"

"No... I like *Beatrice* better. I like how it feels a little more vintage." She leaned back into the seat. "I don't know if it suits me, though."

"Why not?"

Her eyes narrowed. "...I don't know. It just doesn't... *fit*." She was quiet for a moment. When she returned from her thoughts, her eyes found his. Hesitation crossed her face. She blinked and averted her gaze, bringing up her hand to brush away a strand of hair that wasn't there.

"It's okay," Ash replied. "You can ask."

She weighed the question before it left her mouth. "Why did you choose 'Ash'?"

"It felt right," he responded. "I liked that it was short. Kind of cool, kind of modern, not hyper-masc... I liked that it was kind of gender-neutral."

"Did you pick it after someone?"

"Ash Ketchum."

The laugh started in the back of Claire's throat before barrelling through her lips. Ash fought with everything he had to maintain a straight face. When Claire managed to look at him again, his effort had exactly the effect he wanted it to. Her smile fell away. He saw panic enter her eyes as her hand rose to her chin. "Oh... Were you-? I'm so sorry, I didn't mean to-"

"I am one *hundred* percent messing with you."

Her eyes widened. She exclaimed and smacked his arm.

He laughed, unequivocally satisfied with himself. "Careful, you'll scare the horses!"

"*God*, you're awful-!"

"*Aww.*"

"I'm rethinking those gingerbread houses, now."

"*OH-*" He slapped his palm to his chest. "Don't tell me that! No!" He leaned in closer to her and lowered his voice. "I'll make it up to you. Promise."

They looked at each other, close enough that their legs were still experimentally pressed against one another. His gaze flicked quickly from her eyes to her lips, then back again. The seconds grew taut, waiting for a tiny lean or a whispered word to snap.

After an eon, she swallowed and looked away, cheeks even pinker than the cold had left them. Ash leaned back slightly into the back of the bench, every nerve in his body protesting to push forward instead.

"Did you pick your middle name, too?" Claire asked after a moment, fiddling with one of the fingers of her gloves.

"Yes and no," he answered, inhaling. "Not *really*. My middle name was my grandmother's." A pang in his chest where a tube could be. "I just changed it to the masculine form."

"Oh. That's sweet."

"Yeah. I was the fourth grandchild. She kept joking that one of us should be named after her, and everyone got so tired of it that I guess my parents finally did it." The laugh he affected caught in his throat. "She's really great, though. Really funny. Really *vibrant*. I love her. She's actually in the hospital right now. Um-" he caught the sympathy in Claire's eyes- "It's okay- I mean, she's not doing great. She hasn't been for a while. But we still try to include her in Christmas stuff. We visit her."

"I'm sorry. It must be really hard to see her like that."

Ash cleared his throat. His fingers found the back of his neck and scratched at a spot that didn't itch. "Yeah. I mean... yeah. But... it's not really cheerful carriage conversation, so-"

"How long has she been in the hospital?"

He hesitated. "I mean... she was in and out for a little while. But now she's just... in. She's been there for a few months. So it's been a while, it's not a new thing. It took a long time for her to get this bad, but... um. It's tough. Yeah, it's... it's not fun." He retracted back into his seat. More words spilled out of his mouth before he could stop them. "I think it's just a little harder because it can't be helped, you know? It's genetic. So there's really nothing you can do."

"There's nothing worse than feeling powerless to help someone."

"Yeah, exactly."

"Does anyone else in your family have it?"

Ash's noncommittal noise melted into the beginning of a word. "We don't know!" he said through a forced smile. "We don't know. You can test for it, but... it's not really a fun way to spend your day. And who *wants* to know, really? That kind of thing... it weighs on you."

"Would *you* want to know?"

He paused, scratching his nail over the grain of his jeans. "...I don't know."

Claire went quiet. Ash pressed his teeth together. *All of that time making sure she was having a good time and I still managed to fuck it up.*

It didn't matter- he could still salvage it. He took a breath, replacing the smile on his face-

"What do you think would help you live a fuller life?" Claire asked. "Knowing? Or not knowing?"

Ash blinked. One second, she was looking at him in the most gentle way he'd ever seen someone look at another person. The next, she was glancing away, sheepish. His heart sank to see that look leave her face. "I'm sorry, that was *really* personal... I didn't mean to pry."

He guffawed. "No, you haven't. That's the problem. You've barely said anything. And you managed to get me to spill my guts, anyways. You should really consider a career as a therapist. You'd be great at it. Or detective work. Or torture- you'd be great at getting information from people-"

"Are you saying that spending time with me is torture?"

"*No!* No. It's not." He noticed her hand sitting just above his knee. When did she put it there? He pulled the inside of his lip between his teeth. "*It's really not.*"

She looked up at him. A couple of stray snowflakes grazed her eyelashes. "I think maybe you just really needed to talk about it," she said quietly.

It took Ash a moment to realize that he had forgotten to breathe. He was suddenly glad that he was sitting down. *God, how can someone be so pretty?* He brushed a strand of hair off of her cheek, still flushed from the cold. "You're easy to talk to."

He let the tip of his thumb linger at the edge of her face. The corner of her mouth twitched, a slight tug that pulled her lips towards her cheek. He let his gaze linger on her lips until he could feel his heart pattering in his chest. He tore his eyes away to meet hers, looking for permission to pull her closer. He found it.

They leaned towards each other.

The carriage jostled as the horses stopped suddenly, both animals braying and rearing at something in front of them. Ash reflexively braced himself, clutching the back of his seat. He tried to keep from being thrown into Claire as she all but fell across his lap.

He almost had to laugh as he heard the driver calming the horses. *So close.*

He put a steadying hand over her arm. "Are you okay?"

"Yeah, I'm fine. You?"

The horses shifted in place, refusing to move any further. The driver got out of the carriage, taking a closer look at the ground in front of them.

"Is everything okay?" Ash called.

In no particular hurry, the driver turned around and wordlessly started into the forest, trudging complacently through the snow.

8

The driver disappears in the trees. Time passes. They are simmering in each other's warmth. I can taste it. The fear-smell is faint. But it will grow.

I wait.

Her scent swells. Slow. Thick. Sweet. He feels it. His fear prickles to life.

They will cure in that carriage. Alone. In the dark. Together.

The lights dim around them. Slowly. They do not notice yet.

I am watching.

Every look over a shoulder. Every shift in a seat. It makes me want. *Crave. Drip. Drip. Drip in the snow.* It steams at my feet.

He puts his arm around her. He pulls her close. He warns the cold away. Breath makes clouds in the air. Clouds disperse. Grow. *Slow.* Fog in the trees. *Fear.* They stew in fear.

Why do humans fear being alone?

They will not see the teeth. They will not see the claws wanting flesh. They will not see the antlers. The snow-pale skull. The black holes inside. Hunting them. Lusting for juices under skin.

I will make the hunger heel. The hunger will obey.

It knows the hunt is near.

9

"The driver is taking a while."

Claire opened her mouth, then shut it again.

He is?

She is?

No matter how hard she tried, she couldn't quite recall what the driver looked like. She must have been too distracted by Ash's... everything.

She was embarrassed. It wasn't like her to become so oblivious over a guy. "They are," she agreed.

"Seriously, how long has it been? It feels like forever." Ash sighed. "How are you? Cold?"

"A little, but it's okay."

"Did you want my jacket?"

"No no no, it's okay." She looked around again, eyeing the columns of darkness between the trees for any sign of the driver. She waited for her eyes to adjust to the dark like they had before, but as the seconds ticked by, she still couldn't see very well. "Is it just me, or did it get darker out here?"

"Probably just the trees," Ash said. "They must just be really thick here."

She peered into the shadows again, trying harder to concentrate on the feelings of Ash's arm over her shoulders. *You're not alone,* she reminded herself. *You're not stuck.* The horses had quieted down at the head of the carriage. She hoped that they weren't getting cold, standing still in the frigid air. She didn't see them shivering.

Why did the driver leave, again?
"You don't think the driver got lost, do you?" she asked.

Ash made a skeptical face and started to say something, but the words died in his throat. Suddenly, he looked as unsure as she was.

She cast another glance over their shoulders. A light fog had started forming a mesh between the trees, surrounding them on every side. She squinted- something about it seemed strange. *Off.* Fog was... vast. *Billowy.* But this looked... *flat.* It *moved* differently. It *crept.*

She looked at Ash and found him scanning the trees with her. For the first time tonight- the first time since she met him- he didn't have the happy-go-lucky calm that he usually did. He felt stiffer next to her than he had a minute ago. The change made Claire anxious. She had looked to him hoping to find reassurance that everything was going to be okay. Instead, she found her worry found validation.

The dark began to feel oppressive. It closed in on her. The light from the lanterns had felt like a buffer- like space. But they were fading. The oxygen seemed to leave with the light. The dark was infinite and empty... *so empty.*

The quiet. The cold. The memory of car windows starting to fog up and frost over. The handle in her hands that wouldn't open no matter how hard she pulled. A pressure grew in her chest and rose into her throat. *Alone... alone...*

A branch snapped from somewhere in the trees.

Their heads snapped towards the sound.

A figure stepped out slowly from behind the trees. For a split second, the panic had started to subside. *The driver...*

No, she realized. *No, he can't be.*

Looking at him made her want to shiver. He wore a faded, striped scarf over a black double-breasted jacket that didn't look nearly thick enough for the time of year. Dark eyes looked out at them over high, sharp cheekbones. He was thin. *Too thin.* But he seemed completely unaffected by the cold. He hadn't covered himself with a hood, a hat, or an umbrella, but somehow, he didn't have a single flake of snow on him.

"Excuse me-" Claire jumped at the sound of Ash's voice by her ear. "You haven't seen our driver, have you?"

The man regarded Ash carefully, cocking his head to one side. For a moment, Claire thought he wasn't going to answer. "Not for some time. No," he finally said. He spoke slowly, one word at a time, with a voice that lived somewhere between a croak and the creaking of an old, heavy door.

"Do you work here?" Ash asked. "Or do you know the area?"

The stranger considered the question. "Yes. I know it."

The calmness with which the stranger spoke should have been reassuring. But something about his unnatural stillness and the way he spoke- like the words were coming from somewhere *close to* his mouth- left Claire unsettled. She wondered if it was just the anxiety talking. Ash had put on a smile and kept speaking as if nothing were amiss. *Can he really not feel it?*

She shifted in place next to him, her leg still touching his. There was something there- she could sense it. A tension. *He must feel it, too. He has to.*

"Can you tell us how far we are from the market? We hate to leave the driver out here, but..." he hesitated. The stranger started towards the horses, unhurried and unimpeded by the snow. "...They would know the way back, I'd think? And worst case scenario, if we have to walk back..." he looked inquisitively at Claire. She wavered- her stomach clenched at the idea of walking through the woods in the dark. But staying in the middle of the woods in an empty carriage sounded just as daunting. She glanced at the stranger again- He was moving to touch the horses. He removed a thin leather glove and put a pale hand on one of the animals. They didn't react to him. Her gaze lingered on his fingers; they seemed just a little too long.

That was when Claire realized that it was quiet.

Not *peaceful* quiet.

Not the kind of quiet that's muffled by snow, the same way soft voices are muffled by a soft blanket.

It was *eerily* quiet. The horses were silent and strangely still. Now that she thought about it, they had been for some time. There was no sound of birds or crickets. There wasn't so much as a gentle breeze to tousle the branches that crosshatched the sky.

Claire squirmed in her seat. The trees seemed to tower over them, reaching like spikes into a colossal black sky. *When did the trees get so tall?*

"It's rather dark to be walking back without a light," the stranger said evenly.

"It's alright, we have flashlights!" Ash took his phone from his jacket and looked over his shoulder. "And we can just follow the tracks back, I'm..."

He trailed off. She followed his eyes and saw why.

There weren't any tracks behind the carriage. There wasn't any evidence of the path they had used at all. The snow appeared completely undisturbed, and just as thick as it was everywhere else around them.

They had been waiting for a long time. Claire might have believed that the tracks had been filled in by the snow, if it weren't for one thing:

It wasn't snowing.

Wasn't it snowing earlier?

She was certain that it had been.

Snow stopped, sometimes. Of course it did. It was *normal* for snow to stop eventually.

So why did it feel wrong?

The stranger removed his hand from the horse and replaced his glove. He looked directly at them. "I'm able to guide you back." he said. He cast a slow, deliberate glance into the trees. "I don't expect your driver will return any time soon."

"Really?" Ash wasted no time in rising from the bench. He climbed to the ground and offered Claire his hand. "We'd really appreciate it!"

The man stared at them as Ash helped her out of the carriage. After her feet hit the ground, the two men stood there in silence, waiting. Looking at each other expectantly.

She had a sick fluttering feeling in her stomach. *Why isn't he saying anything? Why isn't he taking us back? What does he want?*

The man said, unblinking, "It would be no trouble for me."

"Fantastic," Ash clapped his hands together. "Again, we're really grateful. How far did you say it was?"

"I didn't."

He had a way of not moving when he spoke.

Claire's eyes darted from one direction to the next, landing on the horses. She had forgotten they were still there- they hadn't made a sound. "What about the horses?"

Their heads turned towards her- Ash's a quick snap, the stranger's creepingly slow. She swallowed. Her throat felt dry. Her voice was small. "I don't want them stuck out here alone... getting cold."

Ash had the grace to look abashed.

The stranger didn't remove his eyes from her. "They won't freeze."

She looked back at the horses. Their fluffy ginger-brown coats had collected a smattering of light snow. The tiny bells on their fleece-lined red and green jackets tinkled as they shifted their weight.

She couldn't put her finger on why looking at them made her feel disoriented.

"We can just tell someone at the market about this, right?" Ash stepped closer and put his hand on her lower back. "I'm really sorry," he murmured to her. "Let's get you somewhere warm."

She swallowed again. "It's okay." It wasn't. She didn't know why. But it wasn't.

He flashed her another private smile. "This is going to be a wild first date story, huh?"

Something in her melted a little. "One to tell Kayleigh."

Her face immediately started to burn with mortification. She didn't know what came over her- it just slipped out. Suddenly, sprinting into the trees almost felt less terrifying than continuing to stand there, with Ash- *she could only assume*- looking at her like she was delusional.

She found herself meeting his eyes anyways. His brows had shot up in a flash of surprise. But then the corner of his lips rose into a lopsided smirk, and she found herself twice as disoriented as she had been before.

They turned- the stranger had said something.

"What was that?" Ash asked.

"You may call me-"

He repeated the name. Claire tried to replay the sounds that left his mouth. Trying to recall it, even seconds after it was repeated to her, was like trying to grasp a wisp of smoke.

He was looking at them expectantly again.

She opened her mouth, about to offer her own name out of habit, but Ash cut her off.

"Cornelius. This is Beatrice."

She cringed. *That cheek is going to get him in trouble.*

The stranger regarded them. He looked... disappointed. *Displeased.* The expression was gone so quickly that she wondered if she had imagined it.

"Where are we going?" Ash asked.

The stranger gave him a quizzical look.

"Which direction is the market?"

The stranger pointed. "It's in that direction. Have you been waiting long?" he asked. "I have coffee. If you would like some." He reached into his jacket and pulled out a tall vacuum flask. He unscrewed the cover and flipped it over, the lid doubling as a cup to drink from.

"That's okay, I'm fine," Ash waved his hand in dismissal. "Unless...?"

He looked to Claire. She watched the steam curl out of the flask and into the air. She could smell it from where she was standing. The rich, familiar scent made her wistful. Her hands ached for something hot to wrap themselves around. The thought of a warm drink was a comforting temptation. A small reprieve from the dark and the cold and the man standing across from them who wouldn't quite answer their questions.

She couldn't bring herself to take it. She shook her head.

The stranger put the flask back in his jacket, mouth flat.

"We should get going," she said.

"Okay." Ash took her hand and looked at the stranger. "Why don't you go ahead and we'll follow you?"

"As you wish."

Claire cast a final, concerned look back at the horses as they walked away from the carriage. The snow had accumulated well above their hooves.

She could feel it getting deeper too, starting to seep through her pants and onto her calves as they made their way through the trees.

"So how long is the trek back?" Ash asked.

The stranger didn't look back. "It depends."

"On...?"

He paused. "...Many things."

Ash's next breath came out a little too sharply. "Let's say we move fast and take the shortest route. How long is that?"

The stranger stopped. Claire and Ash followed suit. She felt herself flush again- she hadn't realized until now that she was holding his hand in a vice grip. She eased her grip on him.

"...The snow is thick. Heavy," the stranger said. "That would make it more difficult for you."

Something about the way he said that scared her.

"Maybe we should wait for the driver," she sputtered. "Just for a little longer-"

Ash squeezed her hand. "...I do feel like kind of an asshole, just leaving them there," he agreed.

Claire pulled her phone out of her pocket. *We should call the market for help, or at least look up directions. That's what we should have done in the first place.* She refreshed her browser several times. "Are you getting a signal?" She asked Ash. "Maybe we can just call for help-"

"Yeah, that's a good idea." He held his phone above his head and walked a few steps in a ragged circle. His brows furrowed. He wasn't getting a signal either. His gaze caught on Claire. Her heartbeat quickened again. "Okay, tell you what," he said. "Let's take a look around the carriage, just to make sure the driver is okay- you know, not unconscious or injured nearby or something. And..."

He stopped mid-sentence and looked around. So did Claire.

The stranger had disappeared.

Claire's voice wavered. "Um..." The trees seemed to close in on them. She was beginning to feel like the air was running out around them. She tried to stop the tears from creeping into the rims of her eyes. "Sh-should we-?"

Ash's hand found hers again. "Let's start with checking on the driver. Just in case. Then we'll go from there. One step at a time." He put on another smile for her. "We got this."

They followed their tracks, back towards the direction of the carriage. They hadn't walked for long- three minutes, maybe. It should have been easy to find again.

After almost ten minutes of backtracking, they started walking in small arcs, thinking that they must have angled themselves just a little too far off of the path. When that didn't work, they paced back and forth in perpendicular lines across their own tracks, squinting through the fog between the trees for any sign of equine movement or dim lantern light.

"I was *sure* that it was right here," Ash said again when they returned to a particular spot for the fifth or sixth time.

Claire made no response. She pulled out her cell phone again, hand shivering as she walked in a circle and held it above her head. There was still no signal. She tried to swallow the knot in her throat. "Maybe the driver came back and drove it away?"

"If they did, then we'd see the tracks."

"Unless the carriage wasn't *here*, it was somewhere else."

"I'm sure it was here." A ghost of frustration had slipped into his voice.

"There should be tracks *somewhere*," she countered. "It's dark and the trees all look the same, maybe it was nearby-"

"No, I'm positive that it was here."

"There aren't any tracks here."

"*Yeah, I see that-*" he sunk his teeth into the meat of his lip, biting off the edge of his reply. He took a breath in and let it out through his nose, deliberately slow. "*If* it was somewhere else... wherever it was, I don't think it's here, anymore. We've been looking for how long now? And we haven't seen it anywhere. So maybe it's already gone back."

"As in, the driver came back," Claire replied. *Like I just said.*

"I mean, yeah, or the horses just made their way back or something." Claire didn't think that was likely. But she could feel her nerves fraying and she couldn't bring herself to argue. "If they end up back at the market, someone might come looking for us."

"Or the driver."

"Or the driver, if they're still out here."

"I don't want to wait-" she shook her head- "I don't think we should stay here."

"We don't have to stay right here. We can try heading back."

"Do we even know which direction 'back' is?"

"I think so, probably-"

"I just really don't want to get lost again-"

"It's okay, we're not lost, we're just a little turned around."

Every direction looked the same. They were choked by trees they couldn't even see the tops of. There were no carriage tracks in the snow, and fewer footprints than there should have been.

We're lost.

"I don't even remember which direction we came from," Claire said. "Do you?"

Ash reached up and touched the back of his neck. "I mean- I *think* so. Or close enough."

"'Close enough'?"

"Listen, if we just keep going in one direction, in a straight line, we'll get *somewhere*."

"Or we might get even more lost, if we're not careful."

"So we'll be as careful as we *can* be." He checked his phone for the fiftieth time. "As it stands right now, we have two choices. Right? We can stay where we are- roughly- or we can try to walk back."

She tried to push down the prickling under her eyes. She didn't want to be here. It was too dark, too cold, too quiet, too isolated. She thought she heard some branches rustle behind them. It was getting harder to breathe.

Ash looked at her. "What do you think?" he asked when she didn't respond. "What would feel best for you?"

We shouldn't stay. We shouldn't be here.

This place felt wrong. She was cold. Staying wasn't an option. Neither was getting even more lost.

She opened her mouth.

Something high and anguished cut through the forest. A distant wail snapped either of their heads in different directions. They froze.

Claire was hit with a sickening sense of familiarity.

The worst thing about the sound wasn't the fact that it was the sound of a child screaming.

It was the realization that she couldn't tell which direction it was coming from.

Her eyes regained their focus. She glanced at Ash- he was already looking at his phone again, tapping one finger frantically on the screen. He stopped and looked at her.

She held every muscle in her body as still as she could, as though the smallest movement might make some noise that would obscure the sound of another scream. "We should check on them," she whispered.

Ash's reluctance hit her like a knife in the chest. "...I don't think that's a good idea-"

"That was a *child!*" she cried. "We can't just leave a child alone in the dark, in the middle of the woods-"

"I know, I know- listen-" he raised a placating hand- "we're already a little lost. We can't help them by getting even *more* lost-"

"*We can't just leave them!*"

"*I'm not saying that*- we're in the middle of nowhere! We don't even know which direction it came from-"

"If we just *listen*-"

"We *can't* rely on that, sweetheart, sound travels differently in the woods, it could be coming from *anywhere*." He sighed. "We should try to get back as fast as we can-"

"But we might just get lost doing that anyways!"

"I mean- yeah, but we have a better chance of finding the parking lot than we have of finding that child!"

"Do you *hear* yourself right now?!"

"We *can't* get even more stranded! It's like putting your own oxygen mask on first. Right? We need to get back to the market first, then we can get help. It's the safest thing we can do. For us *and* for them-"

Another scream split the air and echoed around them. Claire shut her eyes and tried to discern a vague direction. The cry tore into her chest and pried her apart until it found a memory- a hollow the perfect size to burrow into.

    She concentrated on the tail end of the scream as it dissipated into the night.

    She opened her eyes. Ash was watching her. His eyes were pleading. He shook his head.

    She turned and ran off towards the sound.

10

The way Claire looked at him before she sprinted off into the trees killed him.

Alarm bells were blaring in his head: *Don't run off into the woods. Don't go towards the screams. Don't look for the child.*

We're going to get even more lost, the rational part of him said.

No, said something deep in his chest. *Claire is going to get more lost.*

The last of his indecision withered and died.

"Wait!" He sprinted after her, chasing the back of her coat.

The ground was uneven, and the snow covered everything. The space between him and Claire grew wider with each clumsy step.

A shape materialized between the trees ahead of him- something disturbingly close to a person.

The stranger's face seemed to stretch and contort; flesh split from crown to chin, birthing blood-slicked bone and a long skull that shouldn't have fit underneath. The jagged tips of horns began to emerge from beneath faded blond-brown hair, ripping scalp from scalp until monstrous antlers grew from the torn remains.

Ash was running too fast. He was charging straight for a double-breasted coat on a too-thin frame. He couldn't slow himself in time. His throat seized as he braced himself for collision. Seams began to rip as he barrelled into limbs that grew too long-

His body never met the creature's. Something battered his ribs as he lurched into the snow. The grunt of pain caught in his windpipe. He started to gasp. Nothing came out.

As the blood rushed to the bruise forming on his side, his throat felt cold. It felt full in a way that a throat shouldn't feel. His hands grabbed at his neck. He strangled himself trying to find the ice inside. Pure cold dripped into his stomach. It was melting too slowly. He couldn't breathe. The cold in his stomach seeped into his other organs. *Freezing cold.* It started to burn.

As quickly as it had come on, the feeling of his body filling with ice disappeared. His lungs devoured the frigid air so desperately it made him choke. His heart pounded and his eyes watered. He raised his head. His eyes ricocheted off of the trees and into the shadows.

The stranger was no longer there.

When he could finally pull himself to his feet, the panic persisted.

Claire was gone.

11

Claire's legs burned.

She stumbled through the woods as fast as the ground would let her, straining to hear over the sound of her own frantic footfalls. She thought she might have heard the child crying again, far away. But she couldn't tell. She might have imagined it.

She tried not to think about Ash.

A child. Alone and screaming. And he chose not to help them.

But he was right, a small part of her whispered. *You know he was right.*

She didn't care. It was too late now.

She wouldn't let that child be left alone like she was.

Between imagined whimpers, she heard the ghosts of more screams. They drew her this way and that, destroying her sense of direction. She lost track of which direction she was going and how far she had run.

Another scream- this one finally more tangible than the rest. It cut straight through the air instead of reverberating vaguely around her. She darted towards it.

The trees that loomed over her abruptly started to thin. They grew sparse around her, briefly less imposing, and gave her a better view of the night sky. Here, she could see that no stars looked back at her from the endless black expanse. No moon hung over her to provide light or direction. When she stopped moving, and the sound of her heavy breathing & exhausted stumbling through the snow ceased, the silence was oppressive. It threatened to drown her, to leave her forever lost & forgotten in an ocean of pine and snow.

She started when she felt small, round *somethings* hitting her forehead and arms. Crude mimicries of holiday ornaments surrounded her, hung from branches with twine, muck-covered ribbon, and worn-out leather cords.

It took her several minutes to catch her breath. The air left her lips in thick, rhythmic plumes.

She took in the scene: The makeshift ornaments dangled from every tree in view, stretching well ahead of her and well behind.

Her chest heaved. She approached one of the decorated branches, chiding herself with every step. *I shouldn't be stopping. I need to get to the child.*

Something about the ornaments unnerved her; they didn't quite look like any of the myriad of trinkets that were sold at the market. They were rough-hewn, yes. *Makeshift.* Clearly handmade. But...

I shouldn't be looking.

The feeling- the sick intuition- blared at the back of her skull. She reached out and cradled one in the very tips of her fingers.

Don't look.

The ball was banded in something like leather. The strip was ragged, as if torn instead of cut, and was beginning to dry and crack in the freezing Winter air.

She twisted the ball in her fingers.

DON'T LOOK.

A clump of hair peeked out from behind the leather wrapping. Something dark and sticky held it in place.

STOP STOP STOP-

There was some kind of faded, blurry print on the leather. Claire couldn't place it. She took out her phone and flipped on the flashlight. She aimed it at the ball.

It was the blown-out ink of an old tattoo.

The ornament dropped from her hand. Her phone slipped from her shaking fingers and plummeted into the snow with it. A horrified gasp came from deep in her chest. Nausea hit her in a wave. She could feel chocolate-and-marshmallow acid knocking at the back of her throat. She stumbled backwards and curled over the snow, dizzy, waiting for it to leave her.

Another high wail sliced through the trees.

It wasn't far. She *knew* it.

With a light head and quivering legs, she pulled herself up and staggered towards the child.

12

The snow holds her scent. Faint. Marzipan sweet. Molasses thick. Hot. *Delicious. Hunger. Need.*

The ball cracks. Crunches under my heel. The rest do not move. There is no wind. Branches are still. Balls hang limp. Dead. Like prey hanging by ankles.

Why hang these?

Understanding prey means better hunts. More kills. More food.

I wanted to understand.

So many skins to wear. To stalk in. Hunt in. And I tore them small instead. Into pieces. To try. To understand.

I could not understand.

I step hard on the ball. *Pop. Crumble. Squash. Useless trinkets.*

There is something else in the snow.

Flat. Smooth. Glass that is black like the sky.

I crouch. Sniff the fear-scent. Taste it.

Yes.

I reach for it. Touch it with my claws. Light flickers. *Light. Sound. Yes.*

I use his fear. Reach for it. Find it in the dark. Pull it. It runs down my foreleg like blood. *Splat, splat, splat on the glass.* The glass drinks the fear like the night sky drinks screams.

It alights. Buzzes like an insect.

He will hear.

I leave the trap. I follow her scent.

13

Ash alternated between glimpses at the snow and glimpses at his phone. He kept the flashlight on to better see the tracks that kept disappearing and reappearing in the snow- none of which, he hoped, were his own- and it was slowly draining his battery. The light shone a wide beam through the fog and created shadows that moved alongside him, slipping over and between the trees, making him jump and look over his shoulder at every turn. He still had no signal. His side ached and one of his legs hurt- presumably another nasty bruise from his fall.

He blamed himself. He couldn't help it.

He shouldn't have been so quick to jump into the carriage. He shouldn't have been so overbearing with Claire. He should have just fucking *relaxed* about everything instead of trying so hard. Now he was asking himself, *was I coming on too strong this entire time? Did I push Claire into the carriage? Did she even want it, or was she just going along with it to make me happy?* The thought tore a hole in his heart.

I'm great at making decisions. Except when it fucking matters.

We should have headed back sooner.

He swallowed the lump in his throat and kept pushing through the snow.

They were going to make gingerbread houses. He was going to make her a mock-charcuterie platter of nothing but holiday treats for them to eat while they watched Christmas movies. And if she still wasn't sick of him, he was going to ask her out again for New Year's Eve.

In all of his plans, he had never imagined Claire taking the lead. She hadn't seemed to want to, and Ash was more than happy to step up. He was a romantic. He wanted to take care of her.

Maybe he was wrong. Maybe if he had tried to defer to her more, given her room to make decisions without his influence, they wouldn't have been in this situation.

His stomach dropped when he felt his phone vibrating. *CLAIRE*. His finger slipped twice as he answered the call and slapped the phone to his ear.

"Claire? Where are you?"

He was answered by a soft, continual static on the other line.

"Claire?" He said. "Hello? *Are you there?*"

He could have swore he heard her voice. It was barely there. He couldn't understand what she was saying.

"I can't understand you- where are you?"

She was answering, he thought. Crying and answering.

"Listen, I can't hear you- I'm going to find you, okay?" He couldn't keep his voice from breaking on the last word. He hoped he didn't sound as weak as he felt. Something in him knew that he couldn't make that promise. But he did it anyways, knowing he had little hope of fulfilling it. "I need you to do something for me, okay?"

He hesitated. He needed her to do what? How would he ask her to help him? By staying where she was and hoping the cold of the small hours didn't reach her before the sun did? Or by playing labyrinth in the woods until no one could find her? Until her disappearance was forgotten and everyone had moved on with their lives without her? Until her face on the *missing person* posts on social media were swallowed by the internet after a few years, just like the trees had swallowed her?

Tears needled his eyes and froze on his skin. He had fucked up. They shouldn't have come here at all. This was all his fault.

"Can you hear me?" He asked. "I can't hear you, so if you can hear me, I really need you listen-"

A scream shot through the trees, its staticky twin assaulting his ear through the phone.

He spun towards the sound. He didn't question that there was a clear direction now when there hadn't been before.

He ran towards it, shouting her name.

14

Humans are not prey.

Prey does not stalk. Prey does not hunt. Prey fears being alone because a pack is safe. Alone is not. Alone is weak.

I have seen humans hunt.

Hunt small prey.

Hunt large prey.

Hunt their own kind like prey.

The trees have drank the blood of predators killed by predators.

Prey fears. Predators do not fear.

Humans fear. But they are not prey.

Predators do not feel fear while they hunt. While they kill. But humans feel fear while they hunt. Kill. Boiling in their flesh or hidden deep in their bones. They fear.

Humans are predators that are not like predators.

Prey fears being alone.

Humans are not prey.

Why do humans fear being alone?

He fears alone. She fears alone. I do not understand.

Rage makes hunger sharp.

15

Ash didn't know why he expected to find Claire in the cabin. He *hoped* he would find her in the cabin. But he had no reason to expect it. There was no light coming from inside, and no footsteps in the snow leading up to the door. Then again, their footsteps had a habit of disappearing on them here.

He looked around and stomped the snow from his shoes, immediately feeling silly for doing so. The floors were filthy- covered in grime and dirt, and scattered with old, dank leaves that hadn't even been swept into a corner. It smelled earthy in the dark, single-room house, with curious undertones of mildew, juniper, stale pastry, and rotting apples. Ash's pulse fluttered. Not wanting to wait for his eyes to adjust, he pulled out his phone and turned on the flashlight. Shadows skittered in every direction as he swung the phone around the room, fleeing and hiding behind the clutter. Tinsel and garlands dried to decrepitude hung from the walls in tangled, irrationally-placed vines. His breath caught as the light hit the far corner of the room- there wasn't anything there. He wasn't sure why he thought there would be.

An austere bed with a dirty mattress was pushed against the wall. Split and broken rails left holes in the footboard, gaping at him like a mouth full of broken teeth. Soiled furs, frayed hand-knit blankets, and filthy ripped holiday-themed quilts lie in a twisted pile on the bed. There were no pillows.

He turned his attention to the large, heavy table that took up almost half of the room. At first, the pieces spread out over the surface made Ash think of a Christmas village. Except instead of cherub-faced miniatures, fluffy polyester snow, and tiny illuminated churches & shoppes, the scene was populated with crude figures and uneven brown structures. Imitations of people were made with twigs tied together with thin strips of discoloured leather, tangled strands and clumps of hair pasted on with long-dried pine sap. A string of tiny lights was propped up by clumsily-placed twigs, standing in seemingly random spots throughout the scene. The cord ended in a dusty battery pack that the creator hadn't bothered to hide from view.

He leaned towards the display- It took him a moment to realize why the diorama felt familiar: The scene was a rough replica of the Market.

He squinted and peered more closely at the scene, he was greeted with the smell of stale spices. His stomach churned with sacrilegious dread: *gingerbread.*

Some of the structures were eroding at the corners, little clusters of crumbs accumulating on the ground around them. A boxy shape that only vaguely resembled a vehicle sat placed in what was meant to be the parking lot. It was topped by a disproportionately long cedar twig, dry and long dead. Nearby, two twig-figures stood side by side, close enough to touch one another.

In a moment of morbid curiosity, he slowly lifted his hand to the battery pack and cautiously pressed his finger into the button.

He wasn't anticipating that the lights would still work- but they blinked to life in front of him, creating a haphazard trail of illumination that snaked around the replica market building before dipping inside via the uneven "door" at the front.

Seconds later, the lights flickered. Ash watched as they faded, quivered, and eventually died.

Apprehension swirled in his gut and put a tang at the back of his teeth. But as he began to turn away, one light in the string- the one that hovered over the attempted car- flickered back to life.

He watched as the lights fluttered on and off, one at a time: over the car... towards the market building... inside the building... slowly, slowly down the length of the inside, towards the back...

Tracking us, he thought with sick realization. *Tracing our path.*

...And just as slowly, back towards the front of the building... out the door... into the parking lot... towards the car...

The light lingered over the pair of twig-figures. Blinked once. Twice. Then moved back to its original place over the car. The single filament glowed steadily for a few seconds before descending into mad, frenzied flickers. The flashes grew brighter and more erratic by the second. Ash quickly pushed his finger into the button again, needing it off. The light continued to flicker and burn. He grabbed the battery pack and pressed the button again- the back of the plastic box opened, revealing the battery compartments. They were empty. He mashed the button over and over as the filament grew too hot and too bright, melting through the gummy-hard plastic coating.

Ash panicked. *It's an LED bulb... a tiny one. It shouldn't be able to burn that hot.*

He yanked the cord from the battery pack. It fell in several places, draped across the scene. The burning bulb dropped directly onto the stale gingerbread car. It smoked on top of the dry cedar branch before setting it aflame.

Ash watched the branch burn and scorch the top of the car.

I'll buy you the biggest tree they have, he had told her. *See if I don't.*

The car shifted and fell apart under the little fire, its side giving way and falling flat on the table.

The hair on the twig-figure nearest the car began to singe and smoke as a needle popped and flew towards it. It started to burn, too.

Ash extinguished the fire with his breath, blowing hard enough to send crumbs and dust flying everywhere.

He drew his phone back towards his chest. It slipped through his fingers, clattering to the edge of the table before falling on the floor, flashlight down.

Ash bent to pick it up. As the light rose and illuminated the floor, it caught a mass of fur half-stuffed under the table. The fur was attached to a folded shape over the floor-

Ash's heart turned to lead.
Not fur.
Hair.

The torn and empty skin of the man they had seen before lay crumpled under the table, sprawled carelessly over the floorboards. Ash retched as he saw the tears in the skin's head, a ragged red rip travelling down the centre of its face.

He started to scream. The sound was choked off as his throat constricted around a surge of vomit. He stumbled against the wall and emptied his stomach.

Another scream ripped through the woods and into the cabin.

Claire's scream.

Ash clambered to his feet and unsteadily bolted back out into the night, still dizzy and twisting inside.

16

Claire felt like she had been stumbling around the forest for hours, circling a voice that ebbed and flowed on someone else's whim. The child's cries were evasive. But gradually, the fog began to thin. The trees grew sparser again, as though the forest was giving itself room to breathe. And the child's voice seemed less like an omnipresent echo and more like a call. Claire followed the sound until it rang clear ahead of her. Relief began to lift the weight from her body. Not just relief at finding the child- although it *was* a relief- but relief that maybe she was no longer alone in what felt like a frozen hall of mirrors.

She could sense it, now- the child was here. Just beyond the next few trees, hidden on the other side of some nearby trunk.

She staggered from place to place, ducking her head around branches and circling trees.

Her foot hit something.

Frost pricked her lungs at her sharp intake of breath. She started to speak, but the apologies died on her tongue when she saw what was in front of her.

She had found the source of the noise. But it wasn't a child that she had accidentally kicked. It was a large stone. The top had been worn almost flat. On top of it sat an old gramophone. The body was chipped in places. The brass horn had been darkened with age. Brown and greenish spots of patina covered the metal like mold.

The child's cries hadn't just been muffled by distance. They had been fuzzy and scratched from the start. They had never come from a human throat, but a nondescript disc spinning far too slowly on a machine that looked broken beyond repair.

Claire sunk to her knees. She dug gloved fingers into her scalp and ran them over her face. The tears were already there when her palms hid her eyes from the trees.

This was what she had left Ash for. This was what she went sprinting off into the woods towards, alone in the dark without any way of calling for help. *This* was what made her feel a stab of disgust for a man who just wanted to keep her safe.

Ash was right. She had no idea where she was.

She stifled a sob with the heel of her hand.

The record started skipping.

The fog grew thick around her once again. It asphyxiated her, tightening her chest with every breath. It became harder and harder to see past the trees immediately in front of her. The child's voice started to speak from the gramophone.

At first, she couldn't understand the words. They were too fuzzy, too drowned in static to discern. But something about them- the rhythm, the cadence of their speech- thrummed inside her. There was something she recognized pushing itself out of the horn.

"...A...*gah-ee*..."

Something told her to run away.

All of her weight had sunk into her knees and rooted her in the snow.

"Da...gah-me..."

She could not stop her ears from trying to unlock the words any more than she could stop the roiling in her stomach.

"Da...got me..."

Click.

She didn't just know that voice.

"Daddy forgot me."

She *was* that voice.

She screamed, squeezing her arms around herself.

"Daddy forgot me."

She willed her legs to move, but her body suddenly felt too heavy for them to support.

She shook, still weeping.

"Daddy forgot me."

Clumps of ice tumbled and fell from nearby trees, shattering on impact ahead of her.

17

Ash didn't know how long he had been chasing after Claire before he found the cabin. When he heard her scream, he didn't bother to think before he ran. He couldn't afford to think. If he did, he might have hesitated. The moment he spent weighing his decisions may have made him a moment too late.

She was too far away. He wasn't going to find her. He was convinced. But he ran, anyways.

He wasn't expecting his body to collide with hers when he saw the fog growing nearly opaque ahead of him, but decided to run into it anyways.

He hadn't seen her- the fog they were virtually swimming in made sure of that. He hadn't heard her, either. She seemed to appear out of nowhere. When they hit each other, the impact sent them both reeling to the ground.

He spat the snow from his mouth and clambered to his feet. He made to look her over, but pulled her into an embrace instead. He couldn't keep track of how many times the questions, *"are you okay?"* and *"what happened?"* left his mouth.

"We need to go," she insisted, her voice ragged. She started to push past him, in the direction he had just come from. Rather, the direction *he thought* he just came from. A fresh wave of nausea washed over him at the memory of what he found in the cabin.

"Not that way-" he grabbed her arm and pulled them in the opposite direction.

They both almost fell over again as she planted her feet and resisted him. "Not that way."

They shared a look. Then they trudged in a third direction, still hanging on to each other.

18

They have found each other. I can smell it.
Fear-scents mix again. Blend. *Ripple.*
I stop. Wait. Breathe the wind.
Prey fears alone. Safer in packs. But humans are not prey.
Fear-scent throbs once. Twice. Then fades.
Perhaps.
Humans hunt humans. Humans feed on humans. Not flesh... rarely flesh. But fear...
Humans in pack feel content because whole pack feels content. Angry when pack is angry. Afraid when pack is afraid.
Perhaps they are a pack.
Perhaps they will feed on the other's fear. *Pack fear.*
The fear-scents fill my skull. Body. Make my stomach feel sharp. Hollow.
It has been so long.
The fog grows. I stalk faster.
Hunt faster.

19

They sat at the crest of a hill, backs against the edge of a towering pine tree. The needles scratched at the backs of their coats when they moved. The forest remained eerily quiet. Claire broke the silence tentatively, feeling as though she was doing something she shouldn't.

"...I'm sorry I ran off." Her throat still felt raw at the edges.

Ash inclined his head towards her, eyes resting somewhere near her shoulders. "I'm sorry I let you."

Neither of them knew what else to say. So they said nothing further.

"...Did you find them?" Ash asked eventually.

She swallowed. She didn't answer at first. "There was no child."

"...What was the noise we heard?" he asked quietly.

"You wouldn't believe me if I told you."

"Try me."

She winced. She had never heard his voice sound like that before. Heavy. *Empty.* Bordering on the bitter. She risked a glance across her shoulder.

He looked haunted.

It wasn't just her.

Her throat felt dry. "...It was me," she whispered. "It was... coming from an old record player. A gramophone. But it was me."

She looked at Ash again. The look he gave her made her want to shrink. He almost reached for her.

"I believe you," he said quickly. "I'm just- what do you mean?"

She hesitated. She was suddenly too aware of the fact that she almost couldn't feel her toes and her fingers were becoming sore in their numbness. "When I was little- about three years old- I was in the car with my Dad. He was taking us home late one night, from a family visit. It was a really long drive, with a lot of backroads. It was close to Christmas. It was really cold out."

She heard a shuffling noise. Ash was starting to take off his coat. She watched him, confused, before she realized that he intended to give it to her. She shook her head and waved it away.

"Take it. You're shivering."

It took her a moment to realize that he was right- she was shaking. *How long had she been shaking for?* She shook her head again.

He was wearing a sweater underneath, but it wouldn't be enough. He *had* to realize that. She swallowed the lump in her throat. *You sweet, chivalrous fool.*

20

The scent is fading. It is getting lost the trees.
Where are they?
How far?
Why is the fear fading?
The hunger in my stomach grows teeth. Gnaws me from the inside. And I do not understand.
My maw stops watering. It foams.
They will not escape.
I will not lose them.
Footsteps in the snow fade. As swift as breath steam. My jaw gnashes the air. I search for scent.
I will tear flesh from flesh.
I will feed.
I will feed.
I will feed.
I will feed I will feed I will feed I will FEED I WILL FEED I WILL FEED I WILL FEED

21

"My Dad pulled over to the side of the road on the way back... It was on a long, wooded stretch of highway, so there wasn't anyone around.

"I don't know why he pulled over... I don't know why he got out of the car. No one does. But he got out... locked the car..." Claire swallowed. *And left,* she thought. *And disappeared. And was kidnapped. And was killed. And ran away. And was attacked & eaten by a wild animal. And stumbled the wrong way in the dark, and died accidentally.* Every possible scenario that had crossed her mind over the decades ran item by item through her head. It was the list she returned to when she lay in bed at night with just a little too much wakefulness left in her to sleep. "I was there all night. Locked in the car. I think he thought he would be right back. He had to." Most days, she believed it. "He locked the doors... But he didn't leave the car on. He didn't leave the heat on. So it got cold. *Really* cold. The windows fogged up, but you could see them frosting over." *Sharp little points of ice, stabbing through the condensation.* Her voice started to break, crackling and skipping between words, as though her mouth was a fluted brass horn and a record was skipping in her chest. Ash's hands found their way to her hand, her arm, her back. "It was so cold... for *hours.* All night. *It was so cold.* And so dark. No one found me until morning, after the sun had risen. Curled up in the back of the car, squeezed into a little ball on the floor between the seats. And no one found him at all."

She went back in time, her body shivering as it had all those years ago, wrapped in too few layers for its tiny frame. Her eyes stung with tears that struggled to come; they had been drained dry over the course of the night.

Every Christmas was a reminder of the father she lost. Every holiday season left her shrinking into herself, trying to make herself as small and unobtrusive as possible. Trying to be less of a reminder for her Papa of the husband he lost.

That had to be the worst part, she thought. Not the endless back-and-forth with the police. Not hearing her Papa leave countless voicemails, asking the officers to do their jobs. Not the way his pleading into the receiver settled into flat, dead-eyed reminders that took less time than it had to pour the glass of rye he needed to get through making the call in the first place. Not the way he looked at her when it started snowing- briefly, like he couldn't bear to linger on her face for too long. Even now, she still had to detach from herself when she looked in the mirror sometimes. The guilt, the grief, and the self-betrayal were all heavy crosses to bear. But they paled in comparison to the perpetual tightrope hurt of *not knowing*.

A therapist once told Claire that closure wasn't something others gave you- it was something you gave yourself. It made Claire so angry that she called a week later to cancel the rest of her appointments with them.

She wished there was a better answer. She wished she could put unquestioning trust in the phantom of her father. But how could she trust a man she barely remembered?

Snow and trees and long, dark highways were just an inescapable reminder that *Daddy forgot me*, the words carved into her throat with desperate little wails.

Ash didn't say anything. He just pulled her head into his chest and held her there.

"I'm so sorry," he murmured into her hair. "I'm so sorry."

She cried like that for some time: cradled in his coat, inches from his heart beating under her skull.

"I shouldn't have brought you here," he said eventually. "I should have taken you somewhere else." She shook her head under his chin. He kept protesting. "This was traumatic for you... Even before that carriage ride. I shouldn't have pushed you so hard. I should have listened. I should have taken you somewhere else. I was trying so hard to make a grand romantic gesture that I didn't listen to you-"

"How could you have? You didn't know. I didn't tell you."

"No. But you were hesitant. And I should have paid more attention to that."

"I *wanted* to come here with you. It's not your fault." She pulled herself up. "I was just anxious."

He was quiet for a moment. "You're so sweet," he finally said. "You're so kind. You're like a little ball of light that just warms up a room." He cleared his throat and wiped under his nose. "And all of this is my fault. Taking you here, the carriage ride, letting you run away on your own... I've fucked it up at every turn. I'm so sorry, Claire. I'm so sorry."

Her lips pursed. *I told you, I* wanted *to be here.* Despite everything, she had *wanted* to be whisked away. She had wanted to let herself see something beautiful in the lights and the snow and the kitschy decorations again. She had wanted him to make her see things differently, if only to make the holidays hurt less. How long had she yearned to find some small joy in the holidays instead of guilt and grief? She wanted him to be that change. That one, magical person that changed everything. She felt ashamed for wanting it. But she still did.

For the first time ever, she glared at him. She couldn't keep the snap out of her voice. "The only thing you're fucking up is making my thing all about you."

He looked down at her, taken aback. She felt a pang of regret. "You're right," he said quietly, "...I'm sorry."

She stared up at his face- plainly remorseful, bordering on panic-stricken. She hadn't seen him lose his composure like this before. She hadn't meant it. Well... she had, a tiny bit. But now that she had said it, she had the urge to wrap him in a hug and tell him it was okay. Which was absurd.

Nothing about this situation was okay.

She could pretend for as long as she wanted. She knew then and there that he already had her forgiveness. She couldn't have withheld it if she tried.

A small cough erupted from her chest. Then another. The more she tried to suppress it, the more the giggle resisted her. Ash's look of confusion only made the giggle grow into a titter, then a full-blown laugh. He pulled away, looking even more panicked than he had before. Alarmed, even. Borderline *petrified*.

"I'm sorry," she said through laughs. And she was, for the most part. "I didn't mean it- I mean, I did, a little bit, but-"

"What's going on?"

"I'm sorry-"

"What's happening?"

"I-"

"Should I- *are you okay?*"

"No, *Cornelius*, I'm not" she lilted.

And then despite himself, he snickered, and started laughing, too.

"*Why- why 'Cornelius'?!*" she wheezed.

"I don't know, because- fucking Rudolph!" Ash exclaimed between laughs. "*Yukon Cornelius! That guy from Rudolph!*"

They were both overcome by another round of cackling until tears ran down their cheeks and they couldn't breathe.

She didn't remember ending up pressed so close to him. She just knew that somehow, after the laughter had started to fizzle, she had.

She thought about how sharp she had been with him, before she ran off into the woods. She thought for the fiftieth time that he was right. She shouldn't have-

Wait a minute.

"...Did you call me *'sweetheart'* earlier?"

He furrowed his brow at her. "What?" Then, gradually, the realization dawned on him. She watched him retrace the night, saw the memory unfold on his face. *"Oh, god,"* he said. She could have swore she saw him flush. "Yeah... I think I did," he admitted. He ran a hand over his face. "It just kind of slipped out," he said from between his fingers. "Sorry."

"Don't be sorry. I liked it."

They looked at each other. Then they pulled each other into a kiss.

22

Scent is gone. GONE.

Faint. Then near. Taste of fear. Taste of flesh. Rich, warm spice, juices, coating my tongue. Near. NEAR. THEN GONE.

Aching teeth. Teeth in belly. Trail of foam, dripping from my maw and boiling on the snow. Breaking branches. Hunger rips my flesh. Claws sharper, legs longer, haunches bigger. Teeth sharper, Spine thicker. Fury fires my blood.

I will find them.

My breath steams. It clouds the air.

No more hunt. No more stalk. Only kill. Only feed. Find. Find. Find find find find FIND FIND KILL FIND KILL KILL EAT FLESH EAT I DO NOT UNDERSTAND KILL KILL FEED KILL FEED FEED FEED I DO NOT UNDERSTAND FEED FEED FEED KILL KILL KILL KILL KILL KILL KILL

23

They were overlapped with one another, wrapped in each other's arms. Ash felt Claire's breathing level out a while ago. He didn't know how long they'd been sitting in silence for. He didn't mind it. Despite the danger and the woods, it felt close to peaceful.

"...What if we don't make it out?" Claire murmured.

Ash turned to look at her- rather, into her hair.

"What if we're trapped in these woods forever?" She hesitated. "It's stupid, but... I keep thinking, what if this is what happened to my dad? He got trapped in some... haunted forest, or *fell through* into some... *place* like this. And he never got out. I keep thinking... what if he died there? Or what if he's still stuck there?"

He gave her arm a squeeze, as much as he could through the padding of their coats. "You think this is what happened to your dad?"

"I know... it's silly. Probably. And I'd think it was nonsense, if we weren't here... But there's something about this place. How the fog seems to have a mind of its own. How your footprints disappear, even when it's not snowing, and the trees get you lost. How you can't seem to remember details about things that happened, and you can't guess how much time has passed. There's something wrong with this place. And it's just been here, this whole time. How many people have been like us? How many people have been lost in here? How many other forests like this one exist? How many are out there?"

Ash stopped himself from shaking his head. He tried to banish the image of the creature's head, bloody and splitting from a torn, skinned face that didn't belong to it. He pushed away the memory of the empty husk of skin on the floor of the hut. "...I don't think it's the forest," he managed. Something spiked in his stomach. He tried to ignore it. "What if we do get out?" He waited. Claire didn't respond. "Indulge me," he said. "What will you do?"

Claire's sigh left her in a gentle, shaky breath. "Hug my Papa. Tell him I love him. Tell Amanda I love her, and my other friends. Get under my blankets or into a hot shower or a bubble bath, and stay there for who knows how long. Book an appointment with a therapist. Regret it when I get there and realize that I can't tell them what really happened. Try painting."

"Painting?"

"Yeah... I've always wanted to learn."

"I've painted a little. I can teach you."

She turned to face him, constrained in her effort not to move her body far from his. "...You're telling me, that this whole time... You could have just taken me to a Painting class or something?"

"Instead of taking us here?" It smarted. But the absurdity of it was more powerful. "...Yeah.

Yeah, I guess so," he chuckled, then grew quiet. "I'm sorry."

"No," she replied. "Of course it was here... It had to be. Of course you drove us forty-five minutes just to take me to the most romantic, festive little place possible to look at Christmas trees and drink hot chocolate on a horse-drawn sleigh ride in the snow. Just to try and make me fall in love with Christmas again." Her fingers made a clunky attempt to lace themselves through his. "That's very... *you*." Ash didn't respond. This *was* all his idea. His grand plan got them here. "...I don't blame you," she said. "I don't. Not at all. Even if you blame yourself."

He could have cried all over again.

"What will you do?" She asked. "When we get out?"

When. Not *if*. He tried to let that small word bolster him. "Spend time with my family," he said. "Tell them I love them. Hug them. Spend more time with my Grandmother in the hospital... try harder to be there for her. Be better for her. Celebrate Christmas... or maybe don't this year." He didn't have a good view of her face. But he could feel the sadness coming off of her. *Optimism*, he thought. *Don't make her feel any worse than she already does.* "But hey-"

She cut him off with a hand on his arm. She gave him a look. *Don't do that,* it said. *Don't pretend.*

He swallowed, trying to brush off the feeling of being caught red-handed. *I was going to watch Christmas movies with you,* he thought. *We were going to make gingerbread houses and kiss under some mistletoe somewhere. I was going to show you what 'Christmas magic' means.* But now the thought of gingerbread houses made him feel sick, and the sweet nostalgia of Christmas movies felt empty.

"Why don't we have a middle ground?" Claire asked. "Just for this year. A compromise. We can do something quiet. Just the two of us. Low-key. We can make it as Christmas-y as we want... Or not at all. We can play it by ear."

"...Okay," he murmured, kissing the crown of her head. "That sounds perfect."

They sat in silence for a while longer.

Claire worried at the top of Ash's hand with the tips of her fingers. "...If one of us gets out and the other doesn't-"

"No," Ash said. "We'll get out of here. Both of us, together." He tried to sound more confident than he felt.

Claire pulled her hand from his. She lifted her sleeve and wiped at her cheek. She took a moment to collect herself. "...Just tell my Papa what happened?" she asked. "As best you can? Please? And tell him I love him. Maybe... just make sure he's okay?" She sounded almost childlike, voice trembling under the strain of trying to keep composed. "He doesn't deserve to mourn his husband *and* his daughter."

No, Ash thought. *No, no, no.*

He tried to lock it out, but she had unleashed the image on him. He felt himself being pulled into its undertow. Having to tell Claire's father what happened- what would he tell him? Surely not the truth? Coming up with a lie that was close enough to the truth to honour Claire's memory... Watching her father, a grown man, fall to pieces in front of him... All while having to contain his own anguish. Having to spend time with this man he'd never met, and now would never be introduced to properly, in the way he should have been, with Claire holding his hand...

He could stay here with Claire. Something about that scared him less than the idea of facing her father and all of the fallout alone. Part of him knew that it would just be a glorified surrender. *Giving up, under the guise of love & loyalty.* But he would be lying to himself if he didn't admit that some days, he felt like a coward underneath it all.

The visions dug their claws into him. Hypotheticals, digging into his brain and refusing to let him go. Getting out of the forest without her... Watching the world keep turning without her... Having to actually move on, remember, find a way to keep living his life, without her...

His heart started pounding in his chest. He couldn't stop imagining Claire's death, and the hundred different ways it might happen. He couldn't stop imagining what it would be like afterwards: living through endless days, going back to a world that hadn't changed while he would never be the same, going through the rest of his life not only responsible for Claire's death, but for her father's loss, her friends' loss, enduring the punishment of living without her-

He barely noticed the shock on Claire's face when he felt the icy burn of something wrapping around his neck. He choked as he was violently yanked away and slammed bodily to the ground. He was suddenly pinned to the snow. Something so cold that it scorched his skin tightened around his throat. He couldn't move. And he couldn't breathe.

24

A scream clawed its way out of Claire's mouth from behind her teeth. Ash twisted on the ground before her. His eyes were wide with fear, mouth shaped like a scream that wouldn't come. A massive, angular creature with a blood-stained deer skull head far bigger than it should have been towered over him, its long limbs still with unnatural ease as it squeezed sharp, slender fingers over Ash's neck. Sharp joints stuck out at unnatural angles, and she could see the severe ridges of its ribs and spine through its pale skin. Claire screamed again. The creature slowly turned its head to face her, mouth leaking foam.

24

Fear-scent explodes in my nostrils.
FIND.
He thrashes in my claws.
KILL.
He chokes. Open maw. Teeth lower. Claws ease.
I taste his scream.
FEED.
She screams.

She could run. *I want her to run.* My legs ache for the chase. Pounding of ground under my feet. Wind on bone. *Tension. Release. Catch and kill. Delicious chase.*

She does not run.

I growl low. *Warning.* She is frozen. I do not stop the growl. The growl builds. Grows. Still she stays. Cries. Screams.

I scream back. Echoes of prey reverberate in my throat. *All prey.* The dying scream of every kill. Small. Big. Bird. Rodent. Animal. Human. Every scream. *Now mine. Forever.* All scream at once, from me.

They are loud. I am loud.

Still, she does not move.

Why?

She fears death. Wants to flee. But there is more fear. Another. *Stronger.*

Rich. Delicious. The *don't leave me.*

I sniff. It soaks the air. All around her. *Don't leave me.* It is intoxicating. *Drip, drip, steaming in snow.* But...

Another taste.
I do not understand.
What is this taste?

I crawl closer to her. She is distressed. The male's body comes with me. Dragged in my claws like carcass. He still struggles. I feel his lungs scream for air. My tongue craves his flesh. Juices. Screams.

She does not flee. Her eyes have frenzy. They watch me. Look to the male. *Stay on the male.*

He is not the one who will kill you. He is not the one who will savour you.

I do not understand.

I throw myself at her. *Stop at almost-kill. I growl. Biting distance. Skull to skull.*

She does not flee.
I DO NOT UNDERSTAND.

I roar. The male goes limp in my claws.

"Why?" I ask her.

She does not answer.

I inhale. *Desperation.* My tongue tastes the air. *Fear of death. Yes. And...*

Don't leave me.
Don't leave me.

I speak again.

"Why... do you... not... run?"

Silence. She stares at the male. She weeps.

She can speak. I know. Yet she does not. "Why... do you fear... alone?"

Quiet. *Timid.* "Please..." she whimpers. "Please let him go-"

"WHY-" *I throw the male.* "DO YOU FEAR-" *I hear a crack. Smell of blood.* "ALONE?!" *Alone* feels strange in my mouth. Her fear makes it strange.

"I don't want to lose him." *more whimpers.* "Please-"

I scream again. She stumbles. I follow.

If she will not run, then she will not escape.

"ALONE!" Not a question. Not anymore. *A demand.*

She chokes. "I don't want to be alone-"

I stalk closer. *"Why?"*

"No one wants to be alone-"

Closer. "WHY?"

"No one wants to be lonely-"

CLOSER. *"What is 'lonely'?"*

She is confused. Trapped. I feel her fear working. The panic races. Singes nerves. Her mind is seeking. Crafting. Failing.

"What is 'lonely'?!"

"I-It's being alone!"

"NO." *It is not. I know it is not. I sink teeth into belly. Coat. Throw.*

She hits a tree. She cries out.

She lies.

She chokes. "It's-"

"'LONELY'!"

"Loneliness-"

"WHAT IS 'LONELINESS'?!" I bite again. Tear. *Rage.* Fabric rips. Shake her. Drop her. I am sick of her riddles. Her fear-scent overwhelms. *Crazes. I*

do not understand and I starve. I crave blood. Meat. Bone. My maw hovers. Open. Close enough to taste. Bite. Rip. It trembles. She does not run. Easy prey for sharp hunger. Too easy-

    I roar. *Lonely.* I have scent of it. But do not comprehend it. It is strange. *Is it poison? Is it delicious? Will it stick in my teeth? Glide down my throat like fat?*

    Will it choke me? As it chokes her?

    She falters. Wet streams down her cheeks. Her heart beats like it is trying to flee her. Abandon her. *Is that loneliness?*

    "WHAT IS 'LONELINESS'?"

    "It's- feeling hungry in your heart! When your heart is starving! Your heart is empty!"

    ...Hungry?

    Loneliness is hungry?

    Is this what can happen from alone?

    Hungry leads to starving. Starving leads to death.

    "Lonely... is starving?"

    I stare. She weeps. She speaks. I do not listen. I think.

    I am hungry.

    Kill-hungry. Feed-hungry. Stomach-hungry.

    Lonely is... heart-hungry.

    I am once hungry.

    I do not want to be twice hungry.

    I growl again. Confused. *Angry.* I thought I would have two meals tonight. *Stomach meals.*

    I am alone. Have I been lonely?

    I have not *felt* hungry in my heart.

Do you know when your heart is hungry? Can you feel it when it is beginning to starve? Does heart-hungry grow teeth like stomach hungry? Or does heart-hungry kill in silence?

I will survive. I will not be heart-hungry.

The male lives. I hear his heart. Quiet. Faint. His fear-scent is faded in sleep. Lingers in the air.

It is cold. He will not spoil. I can return. Feed.

She is still alive. Awake. Afraid.

I carry her in my claws. Her flesh in my jaws is too tempting. She cries. Wails. She does not know where she goes.

I will not be heart-hungry.

25

Claire didn't know how much time passed as the creature dragged her through the snow. The forest already had a way of blurring the line between minutes and hours; the effect seemed to be even more potent in the huge claws of the monster. She tried to pry herself out of its grasp more than once. She didn't realize that she had ripped one of her gloves until her skin made contact with a cold, bony hand, sending a burning shock of ice into the side of her palm.

By the time they reached the cabin, the adrenaline wasn't enough to keep her screaming. She was dehydrated, exhausted, and her throat was scraped raw. Her body shivered, but her face felt hot with tears that refused to come.

The creature threw her into the decrepit wooden building. Her back hit the floor with a blunt thud as the shadow that darkened the doorway contorted. Limbs bent and bones seemed to retract into its body in a jerky series of wet crunches. When it was just small enough to fit through the doorframe, it stalked into the single-room shack towards her. She tried to crawl away, but rammed head-first into a heavy table she hadn't seen behind her. Her cry came out in a stifled shriek as she was lifted into the air by a massive, sharp hand around her scarf-bound neck. The bottom of her jaw was hit with a numbing pain where the fingers touched it.

The next thing she knew, her body was smacking into the wall, chipping the wood behind her. She coughed as the hand constricted over her throat. A pair of void-black holes pored into her from the too-large deer skull, streaked with remnants of dried blood.

The monster's other hand reached behind it. Claire heard a rain of crumbs hit the floor as the hand made its way towards her, stopping short of her face. Fragments of something dry and sticky sat in its palm, turned upwards in offering to her. Its bottomless-pit eyes drilled into her as she glanced over its shoulder. A crumbled ruin covered the table. Pieces of pine, sticks, and wire lay strewn through a mess of brown debris.

Her eyes returned to the mess in the creature's palm. She stuttered without sound. It screeched, shoving its hand towards the lower half of her face. The smell of long-stale gingerbread, acrid sap, and faint hints of mold met her nostrils. The urge to vomit rolled through her. Her cry came out as a strangled shriek. The creature was staring at her, unmoving, and she didn't know how to make it stop. Her limbs started tingling. She could feel her heart in her neck, building a crescendo that refused to stop. Cold started seeping through her scarf. She couldn't breathe.

The monster screeched again, whipping the offering across the room. A hail of decayed cookie fell over the floor, the filthy, broken bed in the corner, and against the wall.

The last thing Claire saw in the midst of her panic attack was a deer skull unhinging in her face. She heard it scream again, an awful sound with an impossible number of voices before she lost consciousness.

26

Food is survival.

Food is debt.

I try to stop her fear. It is too loud. The scent is too strong. Too tempting for the stomach-hunger. My jaws quiver. I want to feast.

I do not feel the heart-hunger. I do not know how sharp it is. *I do not understand.* So I must feed it first.

I give her food. To kill her stomach-hunger. To stop her fear. To make her stay. She will not flee if she eats it. Can not.

Other predators can not give food as a trap.

I am not other predators.

Eaten trap food means she will never flee. Never hide. Trap food will always stay in prey's body. Human's body.

Warm. Cold. Alive. Dead. Close. Far. She will always smell like food.

She does not eat.

Trap food can not be fed by force.

Her fear grows stronger. *Does she know?*

The stomach-hunger is too sharp. *Starving. Rage. Want to kill. Need to kill. Feast.*

I scream.

She sleeps.

I growl. Huff steam in her face.

She drops to floor.

I leave.

I run through snow. Towards the not-hill. The not-nest.

I find it. Between cut-down stumps and dead trees. Near a stream. I hear the water trickle below. Hear it stop. It freezes as I near. It will thaw when I leave.

The hill-nest is mine. It is made of pieces from the humans. Shaped wood. Coloured wood. Broken wood. Metal. String. Rope. Glass. Little pieces of broken things. It is made like a bird nest is made. But it is not warm. Not the right shape to hold young. Not built to stay together.

I watched the hill-nest for many Winters. Waited. Watched it grow. But saw no humans stay. Use it as shelter. Raise their young. Only drop more broken things and leave.

I did not understand.

I take pieces. I build human things. I try to understand.

Winters come. Winters pass. I watch. I build.

I do not understand.

I hunt.

I drop the pieces of hill-nest outside the door. Find good pieces. Leave bad pieces. Wrong pieces. Put good pieces inside. Take sap from the thaw. Push things to walls. Make space.

She still sleeps. I pick her up. *Gentle.* Put her on nest. I must not wake her. I must not tempt the stomach-hunger with fear-scent.

I will make another human thing. I will build it for her. For the heart-hunger. I will try to understand again.
Again.
I will try to understand.

27

It took time for Ash's eyes to flutter open. They felt heavy. A faint ringing faded in and out of his ears as he gazed into the dark early morning sky. It was a very vague gaze- his eyes didn't seem to want to focus for a long time. He was tempted to let himself fall asleep, until he became dimly aware of the snow under his back.

Some part of him was aware that you aren't supposed to sleep on snow. Though the realization felt more like force of habit kicking in than a coherent thought.

He started to get up, propping himself up on his arm, and promptly stopped when a pang of pain throbbed through his head. The ringing came back, easing in an out once more like a wave on the beach.

He shut his eyes and slowed his breathing. An expanse of trees greeted him when he opened them again.

He was in a forest. *Why was he in a forest?* This late, no less. Or this early. *What time was it?*

He pushed himself to sit upright. His head throbbed again, and the ghost of nausea took its time passing through his body. *Ibuprofen. He wanted ibuprofen. Or the other one. Aceta... Acetamorasomething. Acetamanosomething.* He felt his pockets and looked over the ground. He didn't have any.

Fuck.

He sighed, tired and annoyed. *Why am I alone out here?*

He looked over the tops of the trees and into the sky again. There were no stars in the deep blue dark, nor a moon. He figured it must have been early in the morning- five something. Maybe six something.

At least, that was his best guess.

He looked around. *Why am I in a forest?*

Camping, he mused. He would be out here if he was camping.

He turned and maneuvered himself, still sitting, so that his back leaned against the trunk of the tree he woke beside. Thinking was hard. Thoughts kept slipping away from him. Forming them felt like reaching for something on a shelf that was too high.

He shut his eyes and let himself rest a moment. His head hurt. He wanted an ibuprofen. He palmed his pockets. *Fuck.*

He could ask...

Claire.

He could ask Claire.

Right. They were on a date. He drove them out here.

Was he even able to drive right now?

Not out here, he thought. This was the forest. He couldn't drive in the forest.

I guess it doesn't really matter, then.

Claire...

What about Claire?

Oh. Right. They were on a date.

If they were on a date, why wasn't she here? Where had she gone?

Ash hoped that she hadn't left. He hoped she was having a good time. He didn't want her to leave because she was having a bad time. *He didn't want her to leave at all.*

The thought made him tear up. She was so sweet and kind. And maybe sad sometimes. He wanted to make her happy. He liked the way she rolled her eyes but smiled, anyways. He liked her. She deserved to be happy and he didn't want her to leave.

He sniffed and wiped a half-tear from under his eye. He should go find her and make sure she was okay.

He began to get up. His head fought him every step of the way, throbbing anew with every inch he rose. Nausea came and went, but it was weak enough to be nothing more than a discomfort.

He leaned on the tree again when he was able to stand. He felt the cold bark on his forehead and the curve of a root under his toe. He coughed; his throat was sore.

He supposed he could linger there a short while. No one was there calling for him or asking him for anything. He had a few minutes.

A couple tiny fragments of the date came back to him. *Did we look at ornaments already? And trees?*

His leg and his back hurt. He felt like someone had kicked him really hard in the ribs.

Did I get into a fight?
No, I must have fallen.

He looked down at the ground. His body had left an imprint in the snow next to him.

I should ask Claire what happened. Maybe she knows.

He looked out across the forest floor, and saw a mess of massive imprints and something like tracks in the snow. They led through the trees and away from him. Behind him, a misshapen tangle of tracks made their way towards a nearby tree, disappeared around the trunk, and reappeared on the other side before forming the chaotic path away from him.

That's probably where Claire is.

The thought brought a surge of glee and a massive smile to his face- in part due to the thought of seeing Claire again. But more than that, Ash just felt pleased that he had pieced together what felt like a very logical solution. *Just follow the tracks, and I'll find Claire. A perfectly sound plan.*

When the nausea had passed almost completely and his headache dulled, he set out to follow the large, unusual tracks in the snow.

Why am I in the forest?

28

She sleeps.

I have made the human thing. Built it. I still do not understand. But she sleeps.

The sap will grow hard in the cold.

I will not be heart-hungry.

I leave her. The stomach-hunger screams. Ravages. It must be sated.

I must find him.

I run between trees. Bark chips. Branches snap. Claws in snow. Sprays of kicked dirt. Breath steams. Foam drips from maw. *Feed. Feed. Feed. FEED.*

I stop.

He is not here.

I sniff. Pad around trees. I see his body-shape in the snow. Faint scent. Not fear-scent. Body-scent. *Too faint. Too weak.* I growl. I do not understand the human thing I have made. I do not understand *heart-hungry*. I do not understand where he has gone. The hunger gnashes. Emptiness is the predator of all predators.

WHERE?

I scream.

I stalk. Smell the air for fear-scent. It hides. *There but not there. Near but far. I do not understand. I do not understand. The stomach-hunger rips and tears and I DO NOT UNDERSTAND.*

Fear-scent fills my nostrils.

Not his.

Her fear-scent.
She is waking.

I pant. *Drip drip drip on the ground. Steam in the snow. Hissing. Blood. Hunt. Kill. Flesh. Flesh between teeth. Juices on tongue. Fat in throat. In stomach. Hunger sated. Hunger screaming. Kill. Kill. Feed. Kill. Kill Kill Kill KILL KILL KILL KILL SCREAM SCREAM ROAR SCREAM*

She is for heart-hungry. He is for stomach-hungry. Heart-hungry may be silent. Heart-hungry may pounce if not fed. *SHE IS FOR HEART-HUNGRY.* But stomach-hungry is loud. *Stomach-hungry NEEDS NOW. THICK JUICY FEAR AND WARM FLESH AND HOT BLOOD AND DELICIOUS FEAR AND STOMACH-HUNGRY NEEDS NOW.*

I break trees with my bare claws. Snap trunks. Rip branches. Scatter needles. Scream. *Heart-hungry. Stomach-hungry. Hungry. Hungry. Hungry Hungry HUNGRY HUNGRY HUNT KILL FEED KILL KILL KILL FEED*

Scent in the air.
I run.

29

She didn't know how much time had passed before she opened her eyes.

She rubbed her eyes once, then a second time, trying to wipe the blur out of her vision. Her heart fluttered and her muscles stiffened when she realized that her vision was fine- it was the glass that muddled her senses.

The glass was murky. *Dirty*. She could barely see out in some places, and not at all in others.

She uncurled herself from the fetal-like position she found herself lying in. The floor she sat on was made of cold, snow-eroded planks that looked as though they were forced together; cracks and fissures separated pieces of wood in mismatched colours and finishes, some of them splintering. She could feel a hollowness under the board, between the wood she stood on and the actual floor of the cabin. More ragtag planks surrounded the platform in something resembling a circle, with little attention given to symmetry or seam. In an ill-advised moment of panic, she kicked at some of the boards ringing the platform. Dirt scum crumbled off in a couple of spots that looked worse for wear. But they wouldn't move.

The enclosure wasn't big enough to stretch out in. And when she stood up, she could easily touch the glass above her with her hand.

The giant glass orb was only an orb in the most forgiving sense of the word. Massive pieces of thick glass were stuck together with sap, filling the trap with the earthy tang of pine. She traced a sticky, disfigured line between two pieces of glass with her finger. There was something ground into the sap. She couldn't say what. But it gave the makeshift mortar a subtle, spicy smell and an unforgiving thickness that threatened to rip a piece of fabric from her gloves if she touched it.

She spun around, skirting the inside of the glass and looking for an opening that wasn't there. She knocked, then banged on the panes. Her scream for help came out in a breathy crackle. She was starting to lose her voice entirely, now.

Nothing shifted on the outside of the glass. No moving shadows, no creaking floorboards, no shuffling of monstrous feet. She was alone.

The solitude made her want to cry harder. *Abandoned. Alone. Forgotten. Not worth coming back for.*

No. She had to stop the spiral. Or if she couldn't stop it, she had to at least slow it.

Ash was unconscious.

Dead, part of her whispered.

No. Unconscious.

Unconscious, unconscious, unconscious.

She didn't know how much of one's beliefs could really be chosen. But she was doing her stubborn best to choose this one.

Ash was unconscious. The creature was gone. She was alone, as far as she could tell.

The creature was gone.

She took advantage of the adrenaline while she still had it and broke herself out of her head. She started pushing on every pane of glass she could, looking for any possible weaknesses.

After a minute and a half of poring over sap and gauging the varying thicknesses of the glass pieces, she found something- a seam between panes where the sap was applied too clumsily, too sparingly. Like the morbid ornaments she had found before, the trap wasn't made with finesse. It was crude. It was made from scraps and detritus. It may have been meant to hold her, but it wouldn't succeed in keeping her.

She pushed on the glass until her wrists felt sore. She lifted her arm and bent her elbow, bracing herself as she rammed it into the glass. Her coat was in the way- it softened the blow too much. She took it off and tried again, not feeling the sweat leeching into the fabric of her shirt.

She felt the glass shift, but it wasn't enough. She tucked her arm in and charged sidelong at the glass, ramming her shoulder as close to the weak seam as she could. It didn't work. She tried again and again until she was out of breath. The seam had shifted, slipped, loosened, until there was a sticky gap between the panes. It wasn't quite big enough to stick her fingers through, but it was something.

Heaving, she dropped to her knees. She pressed her palms to the wood below her. Her breath came out in raw rasps. She squeezed her eyes shut and thought of her Papa, wondering what happened to his daughter. She thought of her Dad, and the list of *what-ifs* that was growing longer by the hour. She thought of Ash, lying in the snow. *Unconscious.* She remembered the cracking sound she heard when the creature threw him into the tree. *Unconscious unconscious unconscious-*

She rolled onto her back, braced her hands on one of the damp planks behind her head, and kicked.

The pane on the bottom half of the seam held fast... until it didn't. She sobbed, half-laugh, half-cry when it started to give way. The gap between the panes widened one kick at a time, glass opening like a pair of jaws that had been rusted shut.

The pane slanted and came loose. It widened enough for her to crawl through.

She scrambled over herself towards the opening, dragging her coat with her and she climbed over and through the gap-

Her body levitated the moment it hit the floor. Its claws were around her, its roar tearing into her ears. She shut her eyes and screamed a silent scream. It threw her against the wall. She heard the sound of sap ripping and a heavy chunk of glass shattering on the floor.

She finally managed to open her eyes. Her heart nearly stopped with dread.

She didn't know how long the creature had been there. But it had been watching long enough to grab two heavy metal stakes.

She hadn't been alone after all.

In the end, the creature had to tear another three pieces of glass off of the enclosure to get her back inside. It had to reach through the pane she had already kicked away to hold her in place.

Claire watched the glass frost over where the creature touched it. She watched as sharp little points of ice expanded over the panes, closing in on her like a shadow.

She sprained her first ankle struggling to get her leg out of its grasp.

A second massive hand readied a stake.

The pain was excruciating.

She passed out before she could injure herself a second time.

30

Ash's stroll through the trees was more accurately an uneven stagger. He followed the trail of prints until he needed to take a break, got distracted, and came to the same conclusion he kept forgetting: *I should find Claire.*

His head still hurt, and he couldn't concentrate to save his life. But the nausea had mostly passed, and a few more tiny flashes of memory had started coming back to him.

He remembered seeing the carriage. He remembered *sitting* in the carriage, next to Claire. He remembered being close to her, and leaning in...

Had he kissed her?

No. No, he absolutely didn't. There was no doubt in his mind. He never would have forgotten kissing Claire.

He stumbled over a stone half-hidden in the snow, barely catching himself before he fell.

"SHIT- *fucking Jesus-*" He whipped his foot, kicking the stone out of the snow and past a nearby tree. He growled at the blunt flash of pain in his toes when his boot made contact.

He felt his fist clenching of its own accord. It wasn't like him to have such a short fuse.

It was this fucking forest, he decided. He couldn't remember why he was out in the middle of fuck-all nowhere.

Was there a guy, in the carriage? No. Not in *the carriage. But...*

He remembered talking to someone in the forest. After the carriage, he thought. *What did we talk about?*

He reached for the memory- for any snippet of conversation that he could latch onto. But it just wasn't there. All he could remember was a feeling... an unfounded, fuzzy feeling of something being *off*.

There was something strange about that man. *Uncomfortable.* But he couldn't remember what.

He took a leisurely look around him, trying to remember where he was headed. *Why am I in the middle of the forest this early in the morning, again?*

He caught sight of some tracks through the trees on his left. He walked over to inspect them, snapping his fingers a little too hard when he got a better look at them.

Right! I was following these!

He couldn't remember exactly what he was going to find on the other end of them, but he thought it was sound logic to follow them. They might lead him back to the parking lot. Or the carriage.

Did I wander away from the carriage? Is that why I'm out here?

It occurred to him that the best thing to do might be to ask Claire.

OH. Right! Claire- Where was Claire, again?

31

*Hunt. Kill. Feed. Hunt. Kill. Feed. Feed. Feed.
She will not flee. She can not. Not now.
My stomach hungered.
Flesh so warm. Juices flowing. Blood. Butter-brown-sugar-thick fear-scent. Coating my tongue. Stomach-hunger and rage and I made the human thing but I do not understand.
Teeth near flesh. Fresh blood. Kill. Feed.
I must hunt him.
I must feed.
NOW.*

32

The cabin was a decrepit thing, a crusted-over polyp coming out of the snow. Something sat poorly in Ash's gut, discovering that the chaotic trail of prints led here. This didn't look like the kind of surprise find you'd explore during a hike through the forest. This looked like a place to be left alone. *Undisturbed.*

More prints wound around and behind the small cabin, charting other journeys through the trees and back. Large, mis-matched pieces of wood lay discarded in a pile close to the front door, some covered in heavily peeling, festively-coloured paint. A flat plywood pop-up of Santa sitting in a curlicued sleigh stuck out of the refuse, and Ash recognized the shapes of a splintered sled and a broken display board covered in pegs. A smattering of trash was visible between the cracks of the pile, bits of glass and rope fibres sprinkled on top like cinnamon. A snatch of garland drooped over one side, ducking under a piece of wood and disappearing into the mess.

He hesitated. There wasn't any light coming from the cabin, no movement or sound coming from within. That should have made him feel better about peering inside; it was clearly abandoned. But something in the way his feet resisted his attempts to move forward gave him pause.

It's just the dark, he thought. *It'll feel less creepy during the day.*

The logic felt like a reach. The sun was already preparing to rise, turning the sky from a jewel indigo to the colour of dirty water, smeared over with apricot. He looked around, thinking about where he could sit and wait for the sun to come up. His jaw set against the flash of annoyance at having to wait in the cold.

In the cold.

Cold.

He slapped his thigh. *It's cold! Claire hates being cold! I have to make sure she's okay. I have to find Claire!*

He looked again at the cabin, eyes lingering on the warped door. It had been left a few inches open and was practically falling off its hinges. *Maybe it's not able to close properly anymore,* he thought, feeling a small tug of sadness at the idea of someone living that way.

Find Claire.

He inhaled and let the breath out in a pointed, decisive sigh. *It's abandoned. It's just a house. A shed. A few walls and a door. There's no reason to be freaked out. It'll probably be fun to explore for a few seconds. It might be a nice break.*

He set his shoulders and walked towards the door.

It was dark inside- the small windows, few and far between, were covered with tattered, makeshift curtains. The only light that made it in leaked under the fabric and through the boards that composed the wall. Even then, it was early enough in the morning that the light was faint. It took his eyes time to adjust to the dimness. The scent of pine sap and old spices filled his nose, almost enough to completely overpower the hints of mildew and something resembling rotting apples. His feet crunched over leaves that were too grey and too abused to be mere months old. He could feel how caked with muck the floorboards were through his shoes, a constant assault of snow rendering them softer than they should be. He could barely move through the single-room cabin, his path blocked by two massive objects: A heavy overturned table, pushed up against the wall, and an enormous, sloppy attempt at something like a terrarium. Or a crystal ball.

Something made a soft *thunk* against the inside of the glass. The murky, hand-shaped shadow banged an uneven rhythm, growing louder with every hit. His eyes widened as they took in the double-layers of sap between the piecemeal ball of glass, the dark stains on the floor, the patchy garland draped around the tapered wooden base-

Not a crystal ball.

A snow globe.

He choked on Claire's name, swearing when he accidentally ran his hip into a sideways table leg. He peered into the glass, moving around the globe until he could find a patch that was able to see through. A mass the colour of Claire's coat moved inside.

A piece of a memory clicked in place at the same moment another wave of nausea hit him. The strange man, taking them back to the market. *No. Specifically* not *taking them back.*

The strange way he spoke. Something dead behind his eyes.

Where was the driver?

Was he the driver?

He banged on the globe. "Claire?! What's going on?!"

The reply was a wispy rattle. *What's wrong with her voice?* He had to press his ear to a crack in the glass to hear her.

"Help me..."

"How do I get you out?!"

"Before it gets back-"

"Before who gets back?"

He heard her pause on the other side of the glass. That was enough of a reply for him.

"Stand back-" He made a fist and tried to smash the glass. When that didn't work, he tried using his body. He was able to do one weak, aborted launch into the glass before the nausea and the weight in his head told him that was a horrible idea. He heaved, frustrated and fatigued. He backed into the table leg again, jabbing the neighbourhood of his kidney with the end. "GOD *fucking damn it!*"

Claire's gloved palm tapped on the inside of the glass, calling his attention. *"Stop, stop, stop, stop-"* he heard her rasp when he pressed his ear close. She swallowed and coughed, a ragged, pathetic sound that made his heart hurt. *"The glass-"* he saw her

tapping another part of the globe from the inside- *"I kicked one loose- you might be able to-"*
He sunk to his knees and began to pry at the panes where she gestured. Some of the sap was freshly applied, and stretched a little bit when he pulled. But it wasn't enough. It was too stuck together, and his fingers weren't strong enough to pry them apart. *"Shit-"* he tried to dig his fingers into the crack between the panes. They were just barely too big, instead getting smeared with the sap and ground-something mixture that wouldn't wipe off on his pants. *"Fuck!"*
He rose to his feet to look for a solution. A filthy bed sat in the far corner of the room, squeezed in tight by the makeshift globe. On it lay a handful of pelts, torn blankets and quilts, little more than oversized rags in various colours. Lengths of tinsel hung in random strings on the walls, all of them on the verge of falling apart. His feet crunched over something. He looked down- a spray of crumbs littered the floor under him, stretching all the way to the far wall and lodging themselves in the cracks between the floorboards. He knelt, taking a closer look at them. He picked up a couple of larger chunks with his fingers, holding them up to examine them in the morning light that continued to brighten the room at a snail's pace. It was too hard to crumble between the pads of his fingers. *Rock solid.* Something about it tickled the edges of his mind. There was *something* there... What was it?
Crumbling... crumbs...

Claire began banging on the glass again, whisper-calling his name.

FUCK-

His focus was just as out of reach as the memory was.

33

His fear-scent is there.
I stop. *Breathe.*
It is gone.
I charge through the trees. *Break them.*
It is there.
Gone.
Rage.
There. Faint. Quiet. Hidden under something hot. Rage. And her. Hidden under her fear-scent. It fades.
There.
Gone.
Taunting.
TAUNTING.
I smell her. She is awake and afraid. She is there. She is easy meat. Blood. Fear. Meat. Meat. Meat. MEAT. KILL. FEED
I can not feed on her. She is for heart-hunger. I must stop.
Stop.
Stop.
Stop. Stop. STOP STOP STOP KILL FEED
I must hunt him. The hunger will not heel. I can not stop. I will feed on him to preserve her.
Stomach-hunger.
Heart-hunger.
Too much hunger.
There.
Fades. Drowned by hear fear-scent.

Hunt. Kill. Feed. Hunt. Kill Feed Hunt Kill FEED HUNT KILL

34

Claire watched Ash through whatever parts of the glass she could manage. She saw him run through the same cycle several times: He would try to break her out, become agitated, get distracted, and need to be pulled back to getting her out.

She may not have known him for long. But she knew this wasn't like him. She thought back to their last encounter with the creature, and the *crack* she heard when he hit the tree and fell to the ground. The act of replaying the sound in her mind made her stomach roil and her eyes sting.

He was angry. He forgot what he was doing moments after he started doing it. He got distracted at every turn. It had to be a head injury.

Seeing him this way scared her. His irritability made her anxious. But she had to put that aside- she didn't have time to be nervous about his short fuse. He needed medical attention. And she needed out.

"Ash-" she croaked. He remained on the other side of the room, staring at something she couldn't see. His attention only returned to her when she banged on the glass again. *"Try something,"* she rasped. *"If I push, you pull."* She tapped on a pane that he had manage to loosen slightly.

"Okay, one, two-"

She leaned forward and pushed with all she had. She winced when she leaned too far, her face scrunching into a knot as a shock of pain ran up her legs. She felt the glass move by millimetres, fighting against the thick, double-layer of sap that had been applied to its edges.

After three more tries, it stopped giving.

Ash growled, stumbling backwards when he lost his grip. Claire heard something wooden clatter against the wall for the hundredth time. She had to think fast.

"It's okay, it's okay- listen, can you find something to give you leverage?"

"Like what?" he snipped.

"*Something* like *a crowbar-*"

"There aren't any fucking crowbars here!"

"*No, like a crowbar!*" Her voice crackled and skipped. It hurt to talk. "*Like a plank or something! Just something long!*"

"Hold on, let me look-"

She heard him shuffle frantically around the room, push things out of the way, and walk outside. *Outside. Fuck. No, no, no-*

She took several deep breaths that came and went too quickly. She waited. Seconds became minutes. She brought a hand to her mouth to stifle a small sob and tried another deep breath.

He's going to forget you...

"Ash?" She knocked on the glass again. Waited. Waited. Waited some more. *"Ash?!"* She balled her hands into fists and banged on the glass as loud as she could.

She heard boots thumping into the cabin. "God damn it-"

"It's okay-" the tears formed a ball and lodged themselves in her throat. "*Listen, can you find anything?"* He didn't respond. She could feel the hesitation. *"I need you to find a plank or a big stick or something, okay?"* A pause, no response. *"I need you to find something to pry the pane open with, okay?"*

"Fuck-" she heard his voice breaking. "I'm sorry-"

"It's okay, it's okay... I just need you to do this for me, okay? We'll work together. One step at a time." She placed her palm on the glass. It was the closest she could get to touching him. *"A plank or stick, okay? A long plank or stick."*

He sniffed and started moving again. Her heart skipped a beat when she heard him go outside again. She started praying to a god she didn't believe in.

He came back quickly. She heard another wooden clattering on the floor. The air left her body in a gust of relief.

"Okay, you have something long?"

"Yeah, a few-"

"Okay, I want you to see if you can put it in here-" she tapped the crack between the panes- *"just see if you can get the end in-"*

The ragged, broken end of a slim piece of wood started to come through the crack.... and kept coming. He kept pushing it through. She wrapped her gloved hands around it and held it firm.

"No, you're not giving it to me- you're going to use it like a crowbar, okay?"

"I'm sorry-"

"It's okay, it's okay- just put it in this far-" she pushed it out until a handspan's worth of wood

infiltrated the globe- *"And just pry open the glass, okay?"*

The wood leaned back and wedged itself firmly against the sap-lined edges of the glass; she heard Ash grunting with effort. The second time he pushed, the wood snapped and broke.

"Shit-"

"It's okay, I have more-" Another piece of wood, this one thicker, was shimmied and shoved into the globe. It accidentally hit Claire in the arm when it finally pushed its way through. Ash heaved again. Claire took a breath and pushed at the pane, trying to contribute as much extra force as she could.

Push. Give. Push. Give. They were both huffing after multiple attempts, Claire gritting her teeth through the pain as she watched the pane move by scant fractions. Ash swore and smacked the side of the wood.

Push.

The pane rose with a sticky rip, falling and breaking on the ground. Claire could have cried if she wasn't growing numb to her own emotions.

Ash clambered over the glass. She was dimly aware of her name being used- between the heaving and the pain, she was feeling dizzy. She looked up just in time to see Ash's face before her, streaks of dried blood coming from under his hair. *Head injury,* she confirmed internally. He leaned in and pulled her towards him. She yelped in pain as her tendons shifted around the frigid iron. He stopped. Froze. Searched her face.

He looked down.

He saw them, freshly and poorly painted with twisting red and white, peppermint-inspired stripes.

He gaped in horror at the iron stakes piercing her feet.

35

HUNT. KILL. HUNT. KILL.
NO SHARP-CRISP FEAR-SCENT. LOST. HIDING. ONLY HERS. ONLY THICK. JUICY. RICH. BLOOD. FLESH. FEED. FEED. KILL. FEED
THERE
STOP
...
GONE.
Back. It was back. Behind. Towards den. Beyond den. Before den.
Towards den.
I turn. Run. Hunt.
Hunt.
Hunt.
HUNT.
KILL.

36

Ash's stomach lurched. Bile rose in place of words he couldn't find. He couldn't bear the sight, yet he couldn't look away. Drips, splats, and chips of chunky paint covered Claire's boots, confetti over her blood-soaked shoes. A childhood memory came unbidden to his mind- adults telling him and his friends to watch out for nails while they climbed through the abandoned wreckage of a half-finished treehouse. *Don't step on a rusty nail. Are we up on our shots? You don't want tetanus.* He was frozen in place, candy cane stakes coming in and out of focus in his vision.

He didn't realize his ears were ringing again until he heard Claire's rattling voice calling him. She was barely a foot away from him. But her voice sounded so distant, she may as well have been on the other side of a tunnel.

She called again. Put careful, gloved fingertips on his cheek. He blinked hard. Shut his eyes. *"Mm?"*

"I need you to help me out, okay?"

He didn't trust himself to open his mouth, yet. "Mm..."

"I need you to take them out, okay?" she asked.

Fuck-

His stomach churned again. He couldn't stop it this time. He stumbled away, leaned over the overturned table, and emptied what little his stomach could expel. His gut was already sore. It felt empty. This must not have been the first time he'd done this tonight.

Last night, he thought.

He thought.

Running through the forest. Looking for Claire. Dark. Cabin. Something wrong.

He thought.

"Ash-"

He stood again, hearing Claire's weak knocking on the remaining glass.

"*I'm sorry-*" She started.

"What the fuck-"

"I know- I'm sorry, I need you to help me-"

Don't say sorry, he thought as he staggered back over. *Don't say sorry. It hurts. It hurts.*

"*We're going to do this one step at a time-*"

"I got it," he slurred a little too sharply and hated himself for it. It killed him every time she apologized. It killed him that he let this happen to her. It killed him that he couldn't remember how. And it killed him how *fucking incompetent* he was, how full of quick, nebulous anger.

He leaned over the glass and peered down again. He knew he had to grab the stakes. But his hands didn't want to move. It felt polite to brush the chunks of dried paint off of Claire's boots first. Part of him realized what a stupid thought that was. Something about the idea of dusting off her boots while they were impaled by metal rods felt akin to dusting off a dead animal on the side of the road. His repulsion shamed him. Would he feel this way when his grandmother got even worse? How would he handle her funeral? Oh, god, he didn't even know if she wanted an open casket... What if she did? Did he even want to see her like that? Was he ever going to see her without the tubes again? Had he already seen her alive without them for the last time? Was this it for her? Spending the rest of her life choked by plastic, only to find freedom in death? Did she *want* to die? If she did, how would they know? Would she tell them? Ash didn't know if he could tell them, if it was him. He'd be too afraid of hurting their feelings. Was she afraid of hurting their feelings? Wait- that was if she was even *capable* of communicating what she wanted in the first place-

"Ash!"

FUCK. He had been standing there, staring blankly again. Anger flared under his ribs again. *What the fuck is wrong with me?*

"I need you to pull one of them ou-"

"YES. OKAY."

He hated himself.

Using his anger as a catalyst, he forced his hands to reach over the glass. He bent over the panes, getting sap-mortar on the front of his coat as he gripped the spike in her right foot. He felt momentarily light-headed as a little bit of paint came off of the cold metal and onto his hands. He instinctively pulled his hands back to wipe them on his pants, feeling like an idiot all over again. He tried a second time, gritting his teeth and forcing his hands around the metal. Ice bit his skin in seconds, stinging and numbing his palms and fingers. He jerked his hands away a second time, swearing. He felt a hand on his shoulder. He looked up- Claire slipped off her gloves and held them out to him.

Her nails were pink.

She had added tiny gold-glitter accents to the nail on her first finger.

Something in him broke a little.

Swallowing the unwelcome tears, he put on the gloves and gripped the stake again. He could still feel the cold through them.

He did his best to pull straight upwards. He didn't want to hurt her.

I have to hurt her.

He pushed the thought and the guilt away as he gave the stake an experimental pull. She flinched and gasped.

I didn't pull that hard. A tear fell from each eye, now. *I didn't even pull that hard.*

He blinked, squeezing the tears away, and turned to look up at her. She had bit her lip, flesh still pinkish-red where her teeth had sunk into it. She took another unsteady breath and stuffed her sleeve in her mouth. She gave him an urgent nod. He felt sick.

He twisted back towards the spike. He was shaking. They both were.

He took a breath and pulled again.

He heard Claire's guttural yelp muffled by flesh and fabric. His abdomen clenched, threatening to make him dry heave over her feet. The cold-muted smell of iron and blood made him woozy.

The stake was only half-way out.

Claire moaned weakly into her arm. He looked up at her. Her face came in an out of focus. But he saw her squeeze her eyes shut and nod.

He was going to be sick.

No, he fucking wasn't-

He growled as he yanked the stake out of her foot. A small eruption of blood came with it.

Yes, he fucking was.

He rolled his body to the side, hearing the stake drop out of his hand and onto the floor as he fell to his knees and retched again. Nothing but phlegmy spit left his mouth as his organs contracted. He didn't realize until after a couple more heaves that he had put his hand on top of a piece of glass. Plucking it from the bloody gash in his palm felt significantly less distressing than what he had just done.

He still had one more stake to remove.

He didn't think he could do it. He was sure he was going to faint. He hated how fucking *helpless* he felt. *Why the fuck were they even here?*

My fault, my fault, whispered something at the back of his head. *This is my fault, and I don't know why.*

The sides of his face burned as he pushed himself from the floor and bent over the glass. Claire was curved at a strange angle, leaning on the glass to the side of the opening, barely standing.

"Okay?" she asked vaguely. *"Oh my god, I'm sorry... Okay... One step at a time... I need-"*

He wrapped his hands around the stake and pulled.

Claire groaned and fell over as the metal left her foot. Ash realized retroactively that he had screamed as he made that final, sickening pull. He dropped the stake and climbed into the globe, scooping her into his arms.

"Hey-" he cupped her face in his bloody hands. Her eyelids fluttered between opened and closed. "Hey, it's okay- come on, stay with me-"

She floated back from semi-consciousness, mumbling about having to go.

Ash stroked the crown of her head. "I know, it's okay, we're going to get you out of here-"

"*...Need to go now...*"

"It's okay, just take a minute-"

"*...It's going to come back...*"

There was suddenly a ball of lead in his stomach.

"*...Need to go, it's gonna be back-*"

"What's gonna be back?"

"We need... We need to go right now."

"What's going to be back?!"

"We need to go-"

"CLAIRE-"

"NOW."

"Fuck-" he grunted as he got to his feet, helping Claire up with him.

"I don't think I can walk," she whimpered.

"I can carry you."

"Are you sure-?" He bent his knees and put his arms behind her back and her knees. *"I don't think-"*

"YES, I CAN." He stumbled when he lifted her. He was much less steady than his anger had led him to believe he would be. He climbed awkwardly out of the globe and carried her towards the door.

She was right. By the time they reached the pile of trash, he collapsed, taking her to the ground with him.

37

RUNNING HUNT FEAR-SCENT HUNGER KILL FEED RICH FLESH TONGUE NEEDS BLOOD KILL FEED DEN DEN DEN BACK TO DEN FEED NOW KILL FEED HER FLESH HER JUICES HER FEAR KILL FEED FEED KILL-

38

"FUCKING GOD DAMN IT-" He choked.

They both sat there in the snow, panting.

Seconds later, he heard Claire gulp beside him. When she spoke, what little voice she could muster was shaky.

"You need to leave me and go."

He forced himself to bite back something angry. "No."

"I can't walk and you can't carry me."

"I'll figure it out-"

"ASH." He looked at her. Her eyes were red and glassy. *"You need to go. You need to leave me."*

"I don't know how to get back," he protested.

"I don't either. I can't help you."

"Yes you can, you can help me follow the footprints." His argument made no sense. He didn't care.

She looked baffled.

"So, there. You're coming, too."

She swallowed again. *"Ash... there are no footprints."*

"Yes, there are. Look-" he pointed to the mess of tracks all around the cabin. "Footprints."

She stared, squinting. *"No, there aren't."*

"Yes, there are."

"What are you talking about-?"

He gestured wildly with his arm. *"The fucking footprints,* they're all over the place!"

She hesitated, then said cautiously, "...Maybe it's too dark or foggy for me to see, but-"

"What the hell are you talking about?!" he snapped. "There's no fog! The sun is out, it's dawn, now!"

She started crying. His heart broke again.

Jesus Christ, I'm such a fucking asshole, he thought. *What the hell is wrong with me?* He wanted to start crying himself. This wasn't like him. This wasn't what he wanted. This wasn't what he deserved. *Why am I such a piece of shit?*

She started rambling. *"I don't know why you can't see it anymore, but you have to leave- you have to go. I can't leave. I can't walk and you can't carry me, you have to save yourself. That's the only way, you're the only one who can get out of here-"* She put her hand on his chest, another on his face- *"I want you to live- you need to live. Please do that for me? Please go-"*

Watching her father fall to pieces. Watching the world move on without her. Having pieces of her slowly blur and disappear from his memory- her face, her voice, her freckles, the way smiled and rolled her eyes at his jokes-

Never knowing how she took her coffee.

Never knowing what her favourite songs were.

Never getting used to the smell of her perfume or her shampoo.

Never knowing what could have been.

He'd had enough. He shot to his feet and went straight to the trash pile. He had to steady himself before he began rummaging through the refuse.

A big wooden cut-out of Santa and his sleigh stuck out of the pile. Ash grasped both sides and loosened it from the mess, tossing it to the side. Some of the pieces were smaller- planks, splintered sticks, chunks of wood or garland that had been cut from a bigger piece and discarded. Others were massive enough to require both of his hands. He threw those pieces to the side first, trying to find something that would do the job. After a few seconds, he thought that sorting the pieces by size might be a helpful thing to do. So he began a pile of large items where he threw Santa, medium ones directly in front of him, and small, unusable pieces to his right. Some of the wood was painted and peeling. He wondered if it would have been best to sand them down, if he had the time. *Was the paint toxic?* He wondered. *Would I need a respirator to sand it?* He didn't know what the safest practices were for that. He had some relatives who would know. He could ask them. When would he see them? Christmas, obviously, but when would he see them before then? There was going to be another trip to see his grandmother in the hospital... they wouldn't be there, he thought... There was going to be a dinner... *some day... Sunday? One week before Christmas? Two?* He could ask them how make what he needed to make. He stared blankly at the three piles he had made. *Getting the job done. What was the job...?*

    He came out of his trance when he realized that Claire had been rasping his name and crawling towards him.

"*-God's sake, run!*" She cried. "*Get out of here, go back to the market! Go anywhere! It's coming back, just GO!*"

He felt another wave of guilt that he hadn't heard her while he was preoccupied with sorting the trash. He saw the trail of snow smeared with blood behind her- *Oh my god, her feet-* and twisted his head around, eyes darting between the piles and the trees.

She needed to go to the hospital. He would drive her there himself.

She kept whisper-screaming at him to go. He ignored her. His gaze landed on an old sled with cracks in the boards. He strode over, yanked it out of the pile-

"*What are you doing-?*"

"I'm not leaving you!" he shouted.

She sighed, defeated. "*Ash... please...*"

"I CAN'T!" He threw the sled to the ground, its fraying rope landing in a twist on the snow. "I can't leave you! Because I'm just a fucking coward and I don't want to leave without you! I don't want to figure out how to-" he waved his hands- "*do the world* after this without you!" He bent down and pulled on the rope, aggressively dragging the sled in front of her. He pressed the heel of his palm into his eye. "I don't know what the hell is going on. I can't remember half of what happened since we got here. I've been angry and useless and you deserve *so much fucking better than that.* I've been snapping at you and losing the plot this whole time and you've been-" he growled at himself, irritated with his own outburst, but powerless to stop it. *She was the one who was abducted, trapped, and tortured. And she's had to keep it together for* him. The guilt could have killed him. He thought it would, if he got out of this alone.

There were still so many pieces of the night he couldn't remember. But brief glimpses of the past- moments, feelings, words that didn't yet have a chronology- had made gentle, unannounced entrances. The fragmented memories didn't show him that he felt something for Claire; they showed him *why* he felt something for her.

He sniffed. "You are so god damned self-assured. And you're so strong. You're stronger than I'll ever be. And I wanted to be someone you didn't have to be strong around, but-" he interrupted himself with a bitter guffaw- "what, two minutes of talking? Of just sitting there, just looking at me, and I'm already spilling my guts to you, apropos of nothing." *Her hand on his leg.* He talked about his grandmother in the carriage. He knew he did. "It's like... somehow I can just *take it all off* with you. Even when I'm trying not to. And you just- you are *so gentle about it.* You're so *patient.* And *I get it,* I *know* that we don't know each other that well, but I know how you make me feel and somehow I just *know* that you're special, so I don't *care* what it takes, I am *getting you out of here! So get on the freakin' sled!"*

He didn't mean to start shouting. But even now, with a hundred questions and no way to hold the answers, he couldn't look at her without seeing something bright.

She may never want to see you again, he realized. *Not after this.*

It doesn't matter, he decided. He would let that burning bridge destroy him if he got to it. Whether she wanted anything to do with him after or not, he was getting her out.

She looked up at him from where she sat on the ground.

"*...Okay,*" she murmured.

She started to climb onto the sled. Ash immediately stepped over.

"Here, let me help-" He held out one hand and used the other arm to lift her.

"*Just in case we don't make it...*" she said, "*...I really, really like you.*"

He paused, giving himself a moment to keep his voice from faltering. *I really, really like you, too,* he almost replied. "We're making it out," he said instead.

He eased her up and onto the sled. Just as she moved to turn her body one way, he instinctively turned her another. She slipped. He dropped her weight and caught her, but not before she gasped and cried out in pain. In the absence of his arm, her weight had fallen on one of her feet.

"Oh my god, Claire, I'm so sorry-"

She went limp in his arms and fainted.

He scrunched his face into a knot and buried it in her shoulder. He snarled and swore into her coat.

It's going to come back.

Her words passed like smoke through his head.

He lifted her body again and settled it onto the sled. *I'm gonna get you out of here.*

He grabbed a slim, modestly-sized plank from the pile and tucked it in the crook of her arm. *Leverage... self-defense... impromptu repairs... Just in case.*

He looked through the trees for the smoothest or most slippery terrain he could find. He would need all the extra momentum he could get.

He pulled as fast and as steadily as his body would allow him, with no clue which direction he was headed other than a vague "away".

39

-KILL FEED FEED KILL FEED KILL-
STOP
...
GONE
HER FEAR-SCENT. GONE
HIS WHERE?
HERS. GONE
WHERE?
ASLEEP?
GONE???
SCREAM. TO DEN. DEN. DEN DEN DEN DEN KILL DEN FEED FEED DEN DEN DEN DEN DEN-

40

Every bump, rock, and root Ash accidentally pulled the sled over angered him. He let them.

He frequently had to do a double-take of the situation, after his mind wandered and he had found himself dragging the sled along without keeping track of his direction.

Where were we going?

He would turn to ask Claire sometimes, only to find her unconscious.

Back to the car, he thought. *Just get back to the car.*

She fell asleep. Let her sleep.

Wait- I'm wearing her gloves. Why am I wearing her gloves? I should give her back her gloves-

Oh, god, she needs to get to a hospital now-

A sled ride through the snow...

This sled is easy to pull... Or is she just really light-?

FUCK this FUCKING ROCK-

She's so exhausted. Let her sleep.

Fog. Why do I remember fog? Where was that?

I tripped and fell in the snow... and then...

Oh my god, she's injured- how did I forget that, what the hell is wrong with me-?

This must be a damn good sled- hold on... no, it's broken-

Roots are supposed to be UNDER the ground- piece of shit-

Did the trees get shorter? Or are they just different kinds of trees than before-?

"Real gentlemen buy their dates trees." *Pink ornaments. She likes pink ornaments.*

It's time to take her home...

Time to take her home...

He ambled through the forest as fast as his head and the trees would allow. Every exhale left his lips in a puff of mist, reminding him that if nothing else, he was still here.

He hadn't noticed how quiet it had been until he heard a bird chirping above him. He looked up, making a brief, half-hearted attempt to find it as the sun bled into the sky.

EPILOGUE

The girl sat in the bushes. The brittling leaves tickled her face and the branches scratched her arms when she moved. She watched him zoom past her, through the trees again.

"I'm gonna find youuuuu!" her little brother asserted, loud enough to scare some more leaves into falling on the ground probably.

This is why Caden always lost at hide and seek. He was too loud. He didn't understand that it was supposed to be a quiet, sneaky game.

When he was out of sight, she reached for the chain link fence behind her and hoisted herself to her feet. It was probably cheating to change hiding spots, but she hadn't been caught yet. She would cross that bridge when she came to it.

She skirted the outside of the park, careful not to draw her brother's attention. She looked at the playground, beyond the scattering of tawny trees- she saw her sister climb into the bottom of the slide earlier. It was an awful hiding spot. But she was too little to really know how to do strategy, so she couldn't really be blamed. Daddy always said that being bad at something was the first step to being really good at it. When she said that Ava was *definitely* going to be a good hider, then, he just burst out laughing.

She didn't think that made any sense, though. Not really. Because she had things that she was already good at, that she'd never been bad at before.

When she brought this up with Daddy, he just said that those things must be really special talents. Which she guessed made sense, even if she still had some questions.

She ducked into another cluster of bushes when she heard her brother getting close again. These ones were more like hedges than big round bushes, so she was really hiding more *behind* them then inside them. These bushes backed up against the little forest behind the school.

It wasn't a *real* forest... it was too small for that. But she would pretend that it was sometimes when she was younger, playing with her friends.

Her brother sped past again, barely stopping whenever he did look somewhere. She watched him kick through a pile of leaves, crunching with every reckless step. The leaves reminded her of a craft she did in art class two weeks ago. At school they made them do a bunch of different types of art, including crafts and stuff they called "mixed media". She thought it was okay. But sometimes she didn't really know how to put so many different things together.

Drawing was her favourite. If she didn't get to do it at school, she at least got to spend some time doing it at the Arts Centre on Mondays and sometimes Fridays. She even carried a little notebook and a small pencil or pencil crayon in her pocket all day, just in case she got an idea for a drawing. If she had it her way, she would get to be an artist when she grew up. Or a veterinarian. Or maybe both. Mama and Daddy said that she doesn't need to know what she wants to do yet. That was good. She wanted to be a flower shop owner last week, but she changed her mind. She'd wanted to be a veterinarian for longer, anyways. When Mama and Daddy's support dog died, she thought that it would be nice to be able to save animals like him. They told her that he was too old, and that being old happened to almost everybody and it wasn't something you could stop. But she thought that she might like to try, anyways.

That was maybe a year ago now, and they were only starting to talk about getting another dog. One of her best friends at school had a dog who had a surprise litter of puppies. She told Mama and Daddy about that, but they said that they couldn't adopt one. They said it had to be a special kind of dog.

Hmmm.

She heard her brother far away, on the other side of the playground, calling her name. "It's time to goooo!" he yelled. She didn't move. It might be a trick to get her out of her spot. She waited for Mama or Daddy to call for her, to make sure that he wasn't cheating.

A minute later, she heard Daddy's voice calling her.

Okay, then.

She got up and slipped back between the hedges. She ran across the grass and the pavement until she reached the fence and hit the sidewalk.

Daddy was already waiting, holding Ava in his arms. "Come on, Junebug, time to go."

"Okay," she said.

They started towards the parking lot. Ava pulled at the scarf around Daddy's neck, trying to share. That was something Daddy always did- he would pick them up and share his scarf with them when it was cold. She was too big for it now, and so was her brother. But Ava was still little enough to want to. It had turned into a Christmas tradition that Mama would help them all knit, crochet, or sew a new scarf as one of Daddy's gifts.

Some fathers got neckties on Father's Day. Daddy got scarves every year for Christmas.

Some of them were really ugly. She didn't like how sometimes Daddy ended up with a scarf that had mismatched colours or different-textured sections all *Frankensteined* together. It looked *incoherent*. It looked silly. She thought that as a group, they could do better. But Daddy still wore them with a smile, anyways.

Daddy loosened his scarf and draped a long chunk of it over Ava's shoulder. She clutched the edge of it in her little hands and held it close to her face, revealing the stripey scars on Daddy's neck. Daddy kept walking, untroubled.

They followed the fence until they hit the parking lot. Mama and Caden stood at the very edge, watching them come.

"Why aren't you at the car?" Daddy asked. "I got them."

"You're the one with the keys," she said.

Daddy touched his pocket. "I guess you're right," he said with a smile and kissed Mama on the cheek. "Do you want a hand?"

"No, no, I'm okay." Mama squeezed his arm and turned to walk with them, pushing off of her cane. Caden started weaving around the parking lot on the way to the car, like a bee that doesn't know where the next flower is. That gave her an idea- what if there was a bee *made* of flowers? Or a flower made of bees?

No, she liked the bee made of flowers better. A flower made of bees was just silly.

She went into her pocket for her notebook. It's empty.

"Oh no! I dropped my notebook!"

"Did you have it in the car earlier?" Mama asked.

"Yes. I dropped it in hide and seek."

Daddy stopped and put Ava down. She took the scarf with her. "Here, I'll go with you-"

"It's okay, I know where it is. I can get it."

Mama sighed. "Alright, well, be quick."

The girl ran back to the hedge-bushes and walked along the back-side of them until she found her spot from earlier. Just like she thought- her notebook was on the ground. It must have fallen out of her pocket again.

She looked around and found her pencil crayon- pink today- on the ground, rolled underneath the hedge, far enough that she to get on her knees and reach for it. As her fingers touched it, she heard a noise like a branch snapping in the trees. She picked the pencil crayon up and looked behind her. The little not-quite-forest was quiet. She didn't see a rabbit or a squirrel anywhere.

"*Kayleigh!*" Daddy called.

She put the pencil crayon and notebook back in her pocket and ran back to the parking lot.

Kayleigh

She flees from the wood, towards the rest of her pack.

Kayleigh.

Her scent is fresh. *New.* But familiar.

I salivate.

Leaves curl under my feet. Grow cold. Frost coats them like mold. Spreads over the dirt. The chill digs deep in the ground.

I am hungry.

Acknowledgements

Snow Globe was originally intended to be published as part of a collection of short horror stories inspired by Winter and the holiday season. However, as is usually the case with any "short side projects" I start, it spiralled into a story far too big to be contained in a few thousand words.

Thank you to my beta readers, E. Kuhn and Furiosa La Fay. Your insightful, uplifting, and incredibly detailed feedback has been almost as invaluable as your constant moral support. I'm endlessly grateful for all the ways you've supported me, both as a writer and as a friend.

To J.H., thank you for your expertise, both from personal experience and years of medical study & practice. I would trust your waiting jaws with my flesh and my heart without a second thought.

Finally, to D.S., thank you for the occasional brainstorming- and even more importantly- for the inspiration. I still want to make overly elaborate, fucked up gingerbread buildings with you, lover.

Syren Nightshade *(she/her)* is a Canadian author, dancer, singer, actress, & performing artist. She has an affinity for Gothic fiction, and refuses to choose between romance and horror. She unironically loves gift wrapping, and will probably offer to do it for you. She adores festive lights, but detests holiday music. Her favourite Christmas movie is *Gremlins*.